PUFFIN BOOKS
Editor: Kaye Webb

AN EDINBURGH REEL

It was six years since Christine Murray had seen her father go away, so proud and gaudy in his chequered tartan, so strong he could hunt all day and dance all night, and so sure that only a short campaign was needed to put a Stuart on the throne once more.

But now she didn't even recognize the small, hesitant man, so downcast over his prince's defeat and his time in the hulks. And perhaps he was disappointed in her too. Six years of poverty had changed her as well, and a grown young lady in a tattered frock was poor exchange for the excited, well-groomed little girl he had left behind.

Luckily Christine was too busy in the life she now led in Edinburgh, looking after her father, making new friends – especially kind, serious Jamie Lindsay – to spend much time repining over lost prosperity and the Jacobite cause. It was only her father who refused to settle down, and put both their lives in danger by his longing to regain his lost lands and his obsessive hatred of the unknown man who betrayed him after Culloden.

This is a splendidly exciting and lively story set in the bustling, over-crowded Edinburgh of the mid-eighteenth century, with a convincing plot and thoroughly believable characters.

For readers of eleven and over.

IONA MCGREGOR

An Edinburgh Reel

PUFFIN BOOKS
in association with Faber & Faber

Puffin Books, Penguin Books Ltd, Harmondsworth, Middlesex, England .
Penguin Books Australia Ltd, Ringwood, Victoria, Australia
Penguin Books Canada Ltd, 1 Steelcase Road West, Markham, Ontario, Canada
Penguin Books (N.Z.) Ltd, 182–190 Wairau Road, Auckland 10, New Zealand

—

First published by Faber & Faber 1968
Published in Puffin Books 1975

—

Copyright © Iona McGregor, 1968

—

Made and printed in Great Britain by
Hazell Watson & Viney Ltd, Aylesbury, Bucks
Set in Linotype Baskerville

Contents

CHAPTER ONE

Return of a Stranger

CHRISTINE sang to herself as she walked down the street. She sang as loudly as she wished, for the words were drowned in the noise of the crowd that swarmed between the tall grey buildings of the Royal Mile. Six storeys above her head, the washing flapped on the poles like ragged banners, and seemed to be beating out the rhythm of her song; the tradesmen's signs creaked in the wind, and the women screamed down their orders to coal-men and fish-wives.

The evil smells that poured out of the narrow closes and stairways had sickened her when she arrived in Edinburgh two days before. Now she was too happy to mind the stench; the words of the song danced off her tongue, and she laughed when two sedan-porters made her step into the gutter. Today nothing could upset her; her father was coming home.

Six years ago he had gone away to Perth to meet the Prince's army. It would be a short campaign, he said. The Highlanders would march on London, and soon, once more, a Stuart would sit on the throne. Within a few months he would return to Strathdallin, come back to his own house and land, and never have to fight again.

Christine passed the stone crown of St Giles, and the Mercat Cross where they had burned the Jacobite standards after Culloden. The few months had lengthened into six years. For a moment the song died on her lips as she remembered the terrible days after the battle. She had thought the worst was over when they heard that her father had escaped to France. Then news had come of one death, then another, until they heard that only her father was alive out of the six chief tenants of Murray of Strath-dallin. The chieftain himself had been killed at Culloden, and Christine, who had lived with his wife since her father went away, heard night after night the muffled weeping on the other side of the wall, and wondered what they would do now all the men were away. How would they bring the harvest in and dig the peats?

There had been no harvest that year. In June the English soldiers marched up the glen to burn all the crops and every house they could see. Her father's house Tulmore went up in flames, all the crofters' houses, and last of all Strathdallin House. It had made a fine blaze as the soldiers rolled away the butts of claret on the sledges. The crofters' huts were soon put up again – loose stones and bits of turf were easily replaced – but Strathdallin House now had only two rooms where the ceilings still kept out most of the rain, and above those, the charred rafters of the upper floor groaned and swayed in every gust of wind.

The first winter had been the worst of all. After that, a few of the crofters crept back home, and when the Government troops stopped hunting them they scratched out some kind of living. There were no rents for Lady Strathdallin, for the whole estate was forfeited to the Crown, but the tenants came with a hen or two when they could spare them, or a small sack of oats. Sometimes her father managed to send them some money from France. He had been commissioned in Ogilvy's Regiment, and liked his new life, although every letter begged for news from Strathdallin, and fretted against the slow passing of the Acts of Amnesty and Grace that would allow the exiled Jacobites to return home.

It had been terrible to arrive in Edinburgh and find he had not yet come. She had never been out of Strathdallin before except for occasional visits to Perth, when she rode in front of her father to be shown to her grandparents. Her mother had scolded him, saying that Christine was much too young to be jolted up and down in that way.

That was years ago: her mother had died when she was six, and she had never left Strathdallin since her father had joined Prince Charles.

The journey south had terrified her. Lilias and she walked to Perth, then they were met by Lord Balmuir's chaise, which brought them to Edinburgh and the house called Davidson's Land, in the Lawnmarket. Lord Balmuir, her mother's cousin, had arranged her journey and leased the flat for them in Davidson's Land.

Maybe she would have to meet him now that they had come to Edinburgh. This thought frightened her, although she supposed he must be kind since he had taken so much trouble to help his cousins.

Christine pressed her father's letter in her pocket to drive away the black memories. Let them fly away like the scuds of cloud that raced over the narrow slit of blue sky above the Royal Mile. Nothing could go wrong today. As she reached the inn at the foot of the Canongate, she began to sing again.

The October wind was cold, so she stood under the balcony at the back of the yard and watched the stable-boys run in and out, and the caddies, the odd-job men of Edinburgh, spring at every traveller who came into the yard. The travellers were impatient: the coach from Leith was late, they said. If they had to wait another half-hour while the horses were changed for the return journey, they would miss the evening tide.

Christine laughed at their annoyance, too happy to care if the coach came late or early. She wanted to hug her joy as long as possible, until the blissful moment when her father leapt out of the coach and ran to kiss her.

Six years ago he had gone away wearing his belted plaid and bonnet. She had thought then she had never seen such a magnificent figure, proud and gaudy as a cock in his chequered tartan, with the silver-mounted pistols stuck through his belt. He was tall and enormous. The crofters called him 'Red John'. Sometimes they would tease each other with the names 'Red John' and 'Red Christine', because her hair was as red as his own.

But the Highland dress had been banned since Culloden. It was treason to wear it now except in King George's service. No, she must look for him in the French uniform he once sketched for her in a letter. He would wear a blue coat with red facings, and the fleur-de-lys embroidered on its skirt-flaps; he would wear a French officer's sword and his hat would be festooned with gold lace.

She was longing to ask him why he had arranged to meet her in Edinburgh. Did he realize what a crowded, smelly place it was? He would not like it here, she was sure: at Strathdallin he rode or walked all day whatever the weather. He would hunt all day with his cousin the chieftain, then dance until long after the summer light had given way to candles, and still be out the next morning before the sun had cleared the shoulder of Ben Roy.

Out in the Canongate there was a piercing blast on a horn, and three horses drawing a black and yellow coach clattered into the yard. The coachman pulled on the reins, the horses snorted and stamped, and the grooms ran to seize the harness.

The coachman threw his coat in a lordly way to a stablehand, then opened the coach-door, and the passengers clambered out stiffly. There was a clergyman in dark blue clothes and fuzzy bob-wig; a fat woman who panted as she slid her hooped gown through the door; a young officer in scarlet regimentals; and three or four other men. She could not see her father.

Tears of disappointment stung Christine's eyes. She had been so sure he would come. The letter said so. Maybe the packet from Rotterdam had not yet arrived in Leith harbour. She would have to come back tomorrow, and maybe the day after that. Cold fear gripped her. What if he never came at all? But that was nonsense. Her father never broke his word.

She turned away, still half-hoping that the coach was not

yet empty. The passengers were now saying good-bye to each other, as the caddies pounced on their luggage.

There was one man who did not seem to know where to go. He was quite short and small, and stooped a little. He wore a green coat, short-cut in the French fashion, and a dark pig-tailed wig. Underneath it, his hair showed grizzled and sandy. He had no sword, only a small cane. As he came near her, she saw a livid scar on his right cheek. He had a distorted, elderly likeness to her father. But *he* could not be her father, she told herself frantically.

'Christine?' said the man diffidently. 'Are you my child Christine?'

She nodded, horrified, and clutched the tartan screen round her shoulders. It was hard not to back away. Then his arms clutched her so tightly that she cried out what sounded like a greeting. He smelt of snuff and hair-powder, and other strange, foreign smells. When the embrace was over she managed a weak smile.

'Lassie, you've grown so tall!'

Christine gulped and gave a nervous laugh. 'I am fifteen, father.'

'So you will be, so you will.' His glance wavered over her, surprised and uncertain, while Christine struggled with her dismay. The more she looked at him, the more bewildered and shocked she felt.

'Lilias has a meal for you,' she mumbled.

'Lilias?'

'She used to be the still-room maid at Strathdallin. She travelled down with me.' She hardly expected him to remember.

'Aye, I mind on her. Was there room for you both with Balmuir in his chaise? By the way, how is our cousin, Adam Grant – Lord Balmuir, I suppose I hae to call him,' he added with irony.

Christine looked at him in surprise. Their cousin bore this courtesy title because he was a High Court judge, just as Mrs Murray of Strathdallin was known as 'Lady Strathdallin' because she was the chieftain's wife. Although she too was their cousin, and now lived in two burnt-out rooms with hens running in and out of the door, John Murray insisted in every letter that his daughter should 'show the respect due to rank and title'. Surely it was the same with their Lowland cousin. Why should her father sneer because Adam Grant was 'Lord Balmuir'?

She answered his question. 'We didna see him, father. He had to send an agent of the Linen Company to Perth on business. He wrote that I was to meet the chaise with some decent body, and travel so when the chaise returned to Edinburgh.'

'So it wasna such a favour after all!' her father exclaimed. 'I might hae kent it. There's your bonny Balmuir all ower. He'll grease his sheep and grease his bannock with the same pat of butter!'

His violence startled Christine. He went on: 'We'll hae to swallow it. When a man's been out, Christine, he must learn to hae a supple knee and a fleeching tongue. Tomorrow we'll wait on his mighty lordship.' He looked round the yard and waved his stick commandingly at a caddy, who came up at a run and shouldered his leather-bound chest. 'Where's the lodging?' he asked.

'Davidson's Land in the Lawnmarket.' She turned to the caddy. 'It's not long before you come to the West Bow.'

The caddy grinned. 'Lassie, I ken the place fine. It's the tenth close past the Tolbooth gaol. Lucky Robertson and her daddy keep a pie-shop on the ground-floor flat, and Jock Forbes the water-carrier bides in the attics. I'm not so well acquaint with the gentry in the middle. Maybe you'll be leasing old Mistress Lindsay's place on the third floor? The last tenant went out afore Michaelmas. She aye likes to keep the bawbees birling in.'

The caddy chattered without a pause as they followed him up the Royal Mile. Christine was glad that the swarming crowds forced her father to walk ahead. She kept her eyes fixed on his bent shoulders, noticing that his coat fitted badly and was dusty with old hair-powder. Once he fell back to put his arm across her shoulders.

'How blyth I am to see you!' he said. 'You've grown fine and bonny, my dear.'

She was too hurt to feel pleased at the compliment. He was so different from what she had expected. He was a small man, who walked with slow, almost shuffling steps, and even the young children jostled him carelessly as they pushed by. She gave him a tight smile and said nothing.

The crown of St Giles rose behind the Mercat Cross and the buildings pressed even closer together.

'Stick close, sir,' shouted back the caddy. 'It's no far now.'

Two long buildings stood isolated in the very middle of the street. The first was a row of shops and then, higher up the street, there was the Tolbooth gaol. Some prisoners called down from the barred windows and waved their hands; others with white, gaunt faces stared unseeingly across the street. Christine shuddered and stepped closer to her father.

In the Lawnmarket the houses jutted over the pavement on massive stone arches, and the arcades beneath them were crammed with traders' booths. The caddy stopped by one where an old man sat with a tray of pins and ribbons on his lap.

'How's all with you, Daddy Robertson?' he roared. The old man grunted and cupped his ear. 'Where's Jeanie, the day?' The old man grunted again and jerked his thumb at a small opening under the outside stair.

'Yon pig's a gutsy beast,' he complained. 'She eats all day, then she's out snouting again when they throw out the luggies at ten o'clock.'

The caddy peered into the hole. 'She's awful black. She doesna look like Jeanie to me.'

'Yon's a new Jeanie. The old Jeanie went into the pies.'

Christine saw a door in the back wall of the arcade, from

where a fragrant smell drifted into the street. Inside, a woman was moving between the oven and a table where she was rolling out pastry.

'Come on, man,' said John Murray impatiently. Quick as a flash the caddy leapt up the stair before him. 'I'm with you, sir.'

The forestair curved up to the first floor, where it disappeared under an archway in the wall. There it became a complete spiral, with a window on the tiny landing of each floor. Christine became dizzy as she tried to keep up with her father and the caddy.

'The Misses Chisholm,' announced the caddy as they passed the first door. 'They're the ones to ask if the young lady wants a new gown. No sign, as you see. They're ower genty to advertise, but I've never kent them refuse a fee yet.'

On the second floor, he said: 'This is where the Lindsays bide, and old Mistress Lindsay, your landlady. He's an advocate at the Session. They're all away in Fife the now, until the courts take up again. You've another light of the law above you – Lord Niddrie. He doesna sit on the Bench now. He's a wee thing doited in the head, poor old carl.'

They mounted another turn of the stair, then the caddy stopped outside the door and loudly pulled the ring up and down its iron pin. There was a scuffling sound inside, then a long silence. 'While Lilias puts on her shoes,' thought Christine with a smile. Then the door opened, and Lilias, with smiles, and tears, and a gabble of Gaelic, clasped John Murray's hands.

'Och, sir,' she cried at last in English, 'is it yourself come back to us?'

After they had eaten their meal of broth and minced collops, Christine began to feel more at ease with her father. Already that bright childhood memory of him was beginning to fade. As she took him round the four rooms of their flat, and showed him the linen, the crockery, and the well-plenished kitchen that Mrs Lindsay had installed for her tenants, she found her affection warming – grudgingly at first – towards this ordinary, rather surly man who seemed to have lost all his old vivacity and good-humour.

He talked about the voyage from Rotterdam and the dinner his fellow officers had given him when he resigned his commission, but he still did not tell her why he had come to Edinburgh.

At last she seized a moment when he seemed to be in a pleasant mood and asked him directly. He answered her question by pulling a small wash-leather purse from his pocket and shaking a small heap of silver coins on to the table.

'Christine,' he said dismally, 'this is all I have for the three of us.'

She took his hand affectionately. 'I'm a good housekeeper. We can send Lilias back to Strathdallin ... or go back ourselves,' she added hopefully.

John Murray shook his head. 'No, not until I hae my land back again. That's why I'm here, Christine. The forfeited Jacobite estates hae been lying waste for the past six years, most of them.'

'Aye,' said Christine bitterly, as she thought of their unending fight with the stony ground, 'going back to moor and bog.'

'I've heard that some of them are to be leased again from next year. Our fine cousin Balmuir is on the Board of Commissioners that has been appointed to administer these lands. When the Act of Grace was passed, and I could come home again, I wrote him to ask if I could wait on him when I returned. Gey civil his reply was, too. He said he'd be glad to see me, and I was to bring you with me. That's why you're here, Christine.'

She looked unhappily at her stained gown. 'Could you not go your lone, father?'

'He has to hae a pretext, my dear. A good Whig and

Lord of Session canna seem ower friendly with a Jacobite cousin. We hae to humour him, and gie it the guise of a family visit.'

'Pretext?' repeated Christine.

'Aye, that was my word. He kens well that I'll be asking my land back again. Tulmore is only a wee bit of the whole estate. Maybe I'll take the farm that marches with it, forbye. Even the Hanoverian Government dinna want the land to run to waste.'

Christine looked at him doubtfully. She knew nothing about politics, but she thought it could not be as easy as that for an attainted Jacobite to recover his land, even after the Act of Grace.

'Father, do you suppose Balmuir will let – would be able to gie you the land?'

Her father's eyes flashed. 'What way can he refuse? Am I not his cousin? He has an obligation.' His head lifted confidently as he kicked the fire, but there was a note of strain in his voice, as if he were trying to convince both of them. Then he relaxed, and took her hand.

'Come, I hae something to show you.' He led her to his room.

Three of the rooms were in line behind each other, and there was another next to the middle room. It was white-panelled and lighter than the others, and she had at once decided to make it her father's. He went over to his leather-bound chest and brought out a bundle about eighteen inches long.

'I had forgotten that lassies grow tall and become young ladies,' he said ruefully. 'Take it all the same, my dear.'

It was a French wax doll, exquisitely dressed in tiny-flowered blue satin, with red hair and blue eyes. Although inhumanly perfect, its features were not unlike her own when she was nine years old. Christine stroked the smooth cold cheek with her forefinger. She had never owned anything so beautiful.

'Take it away now,' he laughed, as she flung her arms

round him and tried to thank him. 'I'm wanting some peace to write to Lady Strathdallin.' He looked at her thoughtfully. 'Christine, maybe both of us forgot that folk can change in six years.' His face suddenly became strained and melancholy.

Christine blushed and fled, clutching the doll in her arms.

In the kitchen at the back of the house, Lilias was singing softly to herself as she stirred a pot over the fire. She had been tearful and frightened when they arrived in Edinburgh, but she was beginning to recover.

'Is it candles you want, Miss Christine?' She rose and lifted down the two heavy silver candlesticks that Mrs Lindsay had lavishly provided. In future, Christine thought, they would make do with rushlights, but tonight they would celebrate her father's homecoming with Mrs Lindsay's thick wax candles.

She went along the passage to the middle room and put the doll on her bed. Then she pushed aside the curtain that separated her room from the front parlour, and the bright double light caught the painted rafters.

How strange she had never noticed them before. There were plants and trees and fruits, and even grotesque little birds hopping among them. The pattern covered every face of the beams and wooden ceiling. On one beam she read: 'G.D. 1627. In God Is My Traist.' She held the candles above her head, searching for more dates and emblems. Then her father called from his room, and she took one of the candlesticks to him.

There was still a glimmer of light outside. She was drawn to the windows overlooking the street by the sound of carriage wheels, and the bumping of luggage on the stair.

A whole family began to mount the steps. First came a stately old lady in mob-cap and ruffles, who leant on an ebony stick. As she stopped to tilt her enormous hoop through the archway, Christine saw her brocade petticoat and stockings with scarlet clocks. Next came a younger woman followed by two children, a girl aged about seven, and a small boy still in petticoats. Christine smiled as he wriggled from a servant's arms and began to crawl up the steps behind his mother.

Behind the women came two men. They looked like father and son. The younger left his father giving orders to the coachman, and came up the stairs. He glanced up at Christine's window, and she saw he was a boy of sixteen or seventeen, dark and slim, who still wore his own hair.

'What is it?' asked her father behind her. Christine hastily drew back. The boy must have seen her silhouetted against the window when her father came over holding his candle. She closed the shutters quickly.

'Those must be the Lindsays,' he said. 'They're early back. The Court of Session doesna take up for a fortnight.' He laid a large book on the table. 'If you please, Christine, call Lilias ben and we'll hae our devotions now.'

Only once, on the night her mother died, could Christine remember her father omitting their nightly prayers. When she looked forward to beginning their family life again, it was always this moment she thought of.

She drew three chairs round the table and sat with her hands folded in her lap. She felt calm and almost happy. She had been foolish, she told herself, and ungenerous, acting like a sulky bairn because her father was no longer young or handsome. Surely it would not be so hard to accept the sober, everyday truth, after her six miserable years without him at Strathdallin? At least they would now be together.

Lilias came in from the kitchen, and the three of them sat round the table. John Murray opened the Bible, and searched uncertainly through its pages. The sad look was in his eyes again. Christine leaned over to touch his hand.

'It is good to be together again,' she said softly. 'We've not had prayers together for six years, and at Strathdallin we could hardly keep the candles lit to read the Book: the rain kept dowsing the light.'

She could not have said a worse thing. He shut the Bible with a violent oath and threw it on the table. 'Why do you hae to remind me? I try to keep my thoughts clear and still, and ever since I stepped ashore at Leith – oh, Christine, how can I pray or read from the Book when I've got all this hatred in my belly?'

He covered his face with his hands. Christine gave Lilias a look that told her to leave the room, and put her hands on his shoulders. A sick fear began to consume her as she looked back over the day, and remembered all the small, bitter looks and words he had flung at her.

He lifted his head and stared as if she had angered him. 'It's not just to see Balmuir, that I came here. I hae to speak to Captain Binning in the Castle garrison.' Suddenly he grasped her hand and wrung it until it hurt.

'What did I do after Culloden?' he demanded fiercely.

She looked at him in panic and bewilderment. 'You escaped to France.'

'Aye, a year after the battle. I could hae crossed the sea in May, Christine, a month after Culloden. I had friends in Aberdeen, and there was a ship ready. Yon was the worst year of my life, and it need never hae been.'

'Wheesht, now, father,' she tried to soothe him. 'It's all by now. If you escaped after Culloden or a year later, what does it matter?'

His eyes became narrow and ugly as he forced his face against hers. 'You're old enough to hear it now. Four of us took to the heather – two McDonnells, a Stewart of Appin, and myself. They were caught before me. One of them told the soldiers at Fort Augustus where I was hiding. One of them, or someone they told in the camp. Christine, someone betrayed me.' His voice became thick with fury and he began to pace up and down the room with a glare of near-madness in his eyes. 'I was brought before this Captain Binning – he's at the Castle now. I heard from someone in Paris. He laughed when they brought me in. "Give the man five guineas," he said to his ensign. "Tell him his scurvy skin is safe. He told the truth." '

The room began to swim before Christine's eyes, and she sobbed with fear. She longed to run away from the tormented voice, but she made herself stay in the room and feebly tried to reason with his agony.

'Father, how can you be sure? Maybe –'

'I'll find him, I'll find him,' the obsessed voice went on. 'If he's been transported to the Americas, I'll go after him.'

She pulled him to a chair without resistance. It was as if the violent passions in his mind had left his body as weak as a child's. She stared fearfully into his distorted features.

'Father, it canna be helped now. Are we not commanded to love our enemies?' she pleaded.

She seemed only to stir him to greater fury. 'Forgie them, Christine? Did the soldiers that burnt Strathdallin forgie their enemies? Did the English judges forgie the Jacobite prisoners? Christine, if you'd seen us in the transports when they sent us down from Inverness! You'd talk about forgieness, if you'd seen us in the hulks at Tilbury. The stinking offal they fed us on, and the stench, and the lice. Aye, I escaped – but all yon before I escaped –' He jerked up his arms so that the sleeve ruffles fell back over his cuffs. 'Look well, Christine. This is what I got in the hulks.'

His wrists were furrowed with dark red weals that ran in a complete circle round the broken skin, and above the weals the skin was pitted with old sores.

Christine turned away with a shudder, almost retching at what she saw. He thrust his wrists under her eyes again. 'Manacles, Christine, that's what caused yon. I hae more on my ankles. Would you like to see them?' he shrilled.

Then suddenly he dropped his arms, and the fury seemed to ebb away. He looked only tired and sad. 'Go you to bed, now. We hae a journey in the morning.'

Christine took one of the candles without looking at him. She pulled aside the curtain screening the archway of her room. At first she stood still; her mind was empty and exhausted as if she had been out in a roaring wind. Then the numbness began to go. Shudders ran along her cold fingers, until the liquid grease trembled round the candle-wick and spilt on the floor.

The horror of what she had heard began to overwhelm her. She unpinned her gown with shaking hands, and a sob began to swell painfully in her throat. As she stepped out of her gown, she saw the French doll lying on her bed. Its eyes glinted in the candlelight, but the rest of it was still, and coldly perfect. She groped for it blindly as her grief mastered her, and hot tears gushed uncontrollably from her eyes.

CHAPTER TWO

A Visit to Balmuir

'WE shall hire a hackney-coach when we visit Balmuir,' said John Murray the next morning. 'It's ower far to walk.'

'Does Lord Balmuir not live in the Canongate?' asked Christine.

'Aye, during the legal terms. During the vacations he goes to his estate at Easter Balmuir. We hae to make a good appearance. Do you object?'

'No, no,' Christine assured him hurriedly, wishing that her father were not so quick to take offence. He looked her up and down, and she felt miserably conscious of the tears and stains on her dress.

'You'd best put your hair up. You're not a bairn now, and it looks gey wild down your back like that.'

While he went out to be shaved and have his wig dressed, Christine tried to scrub the marks from her gown. But they were old, deeply-engrained stains that would not come out. She arranged the ends of her plaid to hide the worst of them.

The coach drove down the road to Dalkeith, and soon they left the smells of the crowded town behind. Christine took a deep breath of the sweet air through the unglazed windows. These southern hills were low, creeping things compared with the Grampians that loomed above Strathdallin, but it was fine to be rid of the foul atmosphere of Edinburgh.

She knew that she had three cousins at Balmuir. There was a boy of sixteen, and two girls a little younger than Christine. Lord Balmuir had married late, and his wife, much younger than himself, was the daughter of an English country squire.

Christine wondered anxiously if her cousins would make fun of her poor clothes and the way she spoke. They would have fine manners, no doubt, and she would not know how to behave in their house.

'Father,' she asked, 'what do I call them? The young folk, I mean.' Lady Strathdallin was really plain Mrs Murray; but perhaps it would be different with the children of a High Court Judge.

John Murray smiled. 'You surely ken a Lord of Session only has that title as a kind of flourish to his name. The bairns are plain Miss and Mr Grant. Did you not get any education when I was away?'

The heavy joke angered her, though she had promised herself to be forbearing with him today, when he had this important meeting before him. If he stayed cheerful and calm, maybe Lord Balmuir would be disposed to help him. But his remark burnt a slow train of resentment in her mind.

'Mr Nisbet the minister taught me some History and Latin, and a few other things I couldna get at the parish school. I hae no accomplishments.' Her resentment burst forth. 'Lady Strathdallin has had little thought of music, or fine pastry-work, these past six years.'

He smiled at her proudly. 'Dinna fret, Christine. When we go back to Tulmore, you'll hae dancing-masters, and singing-masters, and all you set your heart on. You'll be the most accomplished lassie in Perthshire, I promise you.'

She smiled back, but she did not believe him. He was always full of hopes and promises. That was one thing she remembered about him. Her mind went back to forty-one, the year that the smallpox spread in Strathdallin.

Her mother had nursed Lady Strathdallin and her young son, because the servants would not come near them. Lady Strathdallin recovered, but her son died. Then a week later, Christine's mother fainted as she put her to bed. John Murray ran in as he heard his wife's cry.

'It's nothing, Mary, I promise you. You're weary with

the nursing, that's all. Come out to the air. After a few pints of goat's whey you'll be fine. I promise you.'

Six days later her mother died of smallpox. Time had taken all sharpness from the memory. She could hardly remember what her mother looked like, but she could still vividly hear her father's confident: 'I promise you'.

A blur of houses outside the windows brought her back to the present. They had arrived at the village of Easter Balmuir. These buildings were nothing like the broken-down, turf-thatched huts round her home. She looked in wonder at their dressed stone walls, and the well-kept gardens.

John Murray pointed out of the window. 'See, Christine, Balmuir planned the whole street himself. He's a great improver.'

A quarter of a mile outside the village they came to a pair of high iron gates set between stone pillars. The land inside was divided into fields; not hilly, windy expanses straggling into bog or moor, but small level plots enclosed by hedges or walls. Christine asked the name of the strange crop growing in one.

'They're turnips,' explained her father. 'And do you see the potatoes, over yon?'

She had heard of potatoes, though she had never eaten them.

'What are turnips? Are they good to eat? They dinna look as tasty as kail.'

'It's not the top you eat, it's the *root*.'

'I wouldna like that!' exclaimed Christine. 'See how straight they rise, like rows of wee green soldiers. Look at the stone walls – are they to keep the cattle out? Why can Lord Balmuir not tether his beasts, like we do at Strathdallin?'

John Murray laughed. 'In a wee while Balmuir will turn his cattle into the turnips. He grows most of it for their winter-feed.'

Christine was shocked at such extravagance, when she

remembered their hard-won patches of soil at Strathdallin. 'Father, is it not a shame to see all this good land growing food for beasts, instead of food for men?'

Her father became serious. 'I couldna say. It's the new way. I saw something of the sort when I was abroad.'

The drive now dipped towards a burn and ran through grassy parkland. There were a few old trees, and many more clumps of saplings that would make a brave show thirty or forty years on. The old house, white-washed and massive, with turrets and crow-stepped gables, stood on a knoll by the burn. It seemed to have been turned into some kind of mill.

Almost at the same moment they saw the new house, which still rose starkly from its half-grown garden.

Christine had never seen a building like it. She had not the skill to appreciate the details so meticulously planned by its architect, William Adam. The pilasters, the urns on the balustrade, and the great central Venetian window, were as bizarre to her as if Lord Balmuir had erected an Indian temple in his fields. Amazement drove out every other feeling until the carriage halted on the gravel before the double flight of steps. Then she remembered why they had come.

She stumbled as they climbed towards the entrance, and every stain on her gown seemed twice as large. She felt sick with fright.

The footman stared at them insolently, even when John Murray showed him his master's signature. 'Lord Balmuir is in the library,' he said, as he reluctantly let them through.

They followed him across a heavily stuccoed hall and up a flight of stairs to an antechamber. They heard men's voices through an open door. The footman went inside, then reappeared looking less disdainful. 'Lord Balmuir's factor is with him. He asks you to excuse him for a wee while.'

They sat down to wait. Christine's hands became sticky,

and she kept looking at herself in the gilded mirror. It was amazing that her reflection could look so calm when inside she was in such a turmoil of nervous embarrassment.

'He canna hae the lease unless he plants the trees!' a voice roared from behind the door. There was the sound of a chair moving, and a groan.

'Sir, he doesna want a nineteen-year lease. He'd sooner keep it frae year to year, like his father. He says he'll not hae any truck with English turnips, forbye. He'll just use the mashed straw to feed his beasts.'

'Tell me no more, Davie man.' There was another groan. 'We'll speak about it the morn's morn, when my temper has cooled. Go you now and ask Rob Thompson how the new byres are coming on.'

The factor came out, a ruddy-faced man in slouch hat and boots. He glanced curiously at the Murrays as he walked through.

They heard Lord Balmuir shuffle towards them, and Christine swallowed hard. Then Balmuir half-peered round the door.

'Come away in, cousin John. You'll hae to excuse an old man who is gey heavy on his feet today.' As they entered, he put his gouty foot on a stool with a sigh of relief, and smiled at Christine. He was a vast man, both tall and bulky, and his head looked even more massive in its full-bottomed wig. He wore his neck-cloth twisted through a button-hole in the Steenkirk fashion of Queen Anne's day.

'So you are poor Mary's lassie. You're bonny, but not muckle like her. How old are you?'

'Sixteen next month, sir.' Christine wondered if she ought to have been so exact.

'Indeed. On what day, lassie?'

'The thirtieth of November, sir,' answered Christine, her voice turning to a dry whisper.

'My lord,' said John Murray impatiently.

Balmuir swung round. Since they came in, he had

looked only at Christine. 'Eh? Well, how's all with you, John? Let me call for a glass of wine, and maybe Miss Christine would like a glass of cordial.'

When this had been dealt with, he sat back and smiled at them both. 'My apologies for keeping you outby, cousin. Davie Stuart was with me when you were announced.' He chuckled. 'Come to think of it, it wouldna suit for you to object to cooling your heels for a Stuart, would it?'

'Sir!' cried John Murray indignantly. Christine thought that this was not a very promising beginning.

'Och, dinna be angry. I joked, only. All those ploys are ower for you now. They are ower, are they not?' he demanded sharply.

Murray's face went stiff. 'I am not an active Jacobite.'

Balmuir lifted his hand hurriedly, as if he had probed the matter reluctantly, and was glad to get it over. 'Good. I want to hear no more, for your opinions are your own concern. Now, what can I do for you?'

Christine was glad to see her father's face clear. 'Sir, I hear that the forfeited Jacobite estates are to be leased again.'

'That is so. The Government proposes to pass a bill about them next year. We want to find new tenants to take the leases.'

Murray leant forward eagerly. 'I wish to hae my land – Tulmore – back again. I'll pay whatever fair rent the Commissioners may set.'

Very slowly, Balmuir took a pinch of snuff. Then he said, without looking at Murray: 'What way hae you come to me?'

Murray looked surprised. 'Are you not my wife's cousin, Balmuir?'

The old man pursed his mouth. 'I hae a lot of cousins. The Duke of Argyll is my far-out cousin, and so is Madge Grant that keeps the ale-house in the village. I canna be helping you all.'

John Murray's face became sullen. 'I see I havena the

wheedling tongue nor the honey words you want, Balmuir. If you winna clap hands to a plain request, I canna stoop for any man.'

Balmuir folded his hands across his vast paunch. 'Confound your Hieland pride,' he said genially. 'Dinna take on so, John man. I'll do what I can to help you, but as for gieing you Tulmore –' His voice became serious. 'I hae to answer to the other Commissioners, and the Government in London, forbye. Your request isna reasonable.'

The words were neither kind nor unkind, but spoken as a simple truth. 'He's right,' thought Christine. 'Even a bairn could see it. My father was daft to ask him.'

'Can you not recommend a man as a tenant?' persisted Murray.

'Aye, if he's fit.'

Murray said bitterly: 'Naturally, no Jacobite is fit.'

.'*You* are not fit.' Balmuir emphasized his words with a finger jabbing the table. 'Imprimis, you're new home from France, and fair words of loyalty to King George are not enough to convince us. Anyways, you're too ignorant to hold the land, be you Whig or Jacobite.'

Murray protested. 'A man doesna forget his old skills in six years.'

'Tchah! Your old skills are older than Gog and Magog. We want to see these forfeited estates let out to improving tenants. Look at you, before the Rising: your marshy, unfenced fields, your miserable runts that looked liker rats nor cattle when you drove them to the Crieff tryst!'

'The land in the north is ill to farm, Balmuir.'

'Maybe. But what would you care for drainage and enclosures, or rotating your crops, even if you kent how to do it? You hae no interest in improving your land. I doubt you've never heard of rye-grass or clover.'

John Murray heard him with tight lips, his eyes smouldering. Balmuir held up his hand.

'Wheesht, I'm not done yet. As to Tulmore, and the whole of Strathdallin, there's another matter. The Linen

Company want to grow flax there – acres and acres of it. We're going to set up a heckling mill and a spinning-school there, where the lassies can learn to spin the French way and learn their letters at the same time.'

'Flax! Linen!' John Murray was aghast. Balmuir frowned.

'Is it not better for them to be at their wheels than carrying farm-dung to the fields on their backs? Maybe when they sold the linen yarn they could buy a pony to carry the dung for them.'

Christine saw her father's anger change into bewildered despair. 'The land belongs to the Murrays of Strath-dallin. You canna change our lives like this.'

Balmuir was unmoved. 'You tacksmen care only for your rents. Your tenants live no better than beasts in their dirty wee houses. We want to help them. Not one bawbee from these estates will go out of Scotland. The rents will all be spent on improvement.'

'You've taken away our Highland dress,' said Murray bitterly, 'and the power of our chieftains. Now you want to steal our land.'

Balmuir thumped his chair in exasperation. 'John, if you dinna bend your backs to the new ways, there are others that will drive you off your precious land.'

'Who would they be, if not yourselves?' asked Murray. 'The sheep.'

John Murray rose impatiently. 'I must ask your leave to go, my lord,' he said formally. 'We are wasting each other's time.'

At once the old man's severity vanished. 'Dinna go so soon. Let you and me take a dander round the policies till dinner-time, while Christine goes to meet the womenfolk.'

Christine looked at her father. The grandeur of the house frightened her; she longed to go back to Edinburgh. She could see her father was smarting under Balmuir's refusal, and the longer they stayed the more his pride would be hurt. Yet there might be other ways in which

Balmuir could help them; it would be wise to humour him.

'I'd like fine to meet my cousins, father,' she said.

Balmuir looked pleased. 'That's settled, then,' he said.

The footman took her in haughty silence to the house-keeper, who was counting two enormous piles of linen and napery. After a few words of annoyance at being inter-rupted in her work, she took Christine to the music-room.

The tight feeling inside Christine grew worse as they went along more corridors and galleries and stairs, and the housemaids ducked out of their path with stifled giggles at Christine's shabby gown. She felt her cheeks burn, but she walked proudly past them, determined not to let them see how uncomfortable she felt.

Another servant must have gone ahead of them. The four occupants of the music-room showed no surprise when the housekeeper showed her in. Lady Balmuir sewed while one of her daughters played the harpsichord, and the other sang to her sister's accompaniment. Over them, with one silken leg crossing the other, hung a small, swarthy man with a look of rapture on his face.

'Thank you, Signor Rosalbo,' said Lady Balmuir gra-ciously. 'We shall conclude the lesson now.' She beckoned Christine to sit beside her, but there was no warmth in her gesture. Christine held her woollen gown away from Lady Balmuir's French silks as she sat down.

'Well, my dear,' said Lady Balmuir after the music-master had left them, 'it must be a great comfort that your father has returned from France.' Her intonation was pleasant, but sounded strange to Christine, who had never heard an English voice before. 'Do you intend to stay long in Edinburgh?'

Christine tried to meet the cool glance, but dropped her eyes and stammered: 'I dinna ken. My father has busi-ness in Edinburgh, but he hasna said how long it will take him.'

'Perhaps we shall see more of you,' said Lady Balmuir. 'We shall return to town soon for the winter Session.'

Christine saw her cousins watching her with excited curiosity. Like their mother, they were fair and delicately featured. The younger, whom Lady Balmuir had introduced as 'Henrietta', fidgeted impatiently while her mother was in the room. In a few moments, Lady Balmuir gathered up her tambour-frame and said that she would leave the three of them to become better acquainted: she would see Christine again when her cousins brought her to dinner.

Christine smiled hopefully at her cousins, but was too shy to speak first. Elizabeth, the elder, frowned at Christine's faded gown. 'Are you really our cousin?' she asked.

Henrietta's eyes gleamed. 'Of course she is. She's our *Jacobite* cousin. Papa says the Jacobites are traitors.' She watched Christine closely as she said this.

Christine flushed. She thought of the way the crofters' children would catch a blackbird in a basket, then poke it with a straw; not really meaning to be cruel, but wanting to find out what the creature would do in its strange surroundings. For her father's sake, she would not let them make her angry. 'My father has been pardoned,' she said quietly.

They circled round her; their curiosity was so impersonal that Christine ceased to be embarrassed.

'How brown your face and hands are!' exclaimed Henrietta. 'Anybody would think you'd been working in the fields.'

Christine's chin lifted pugnaciously. 'So I have.'

They stared at her in horror. 'D'you not leave that to the servants?'

She laughed contemptuously at their ignorance. 'There are hardly any men to do the work for us. Most of them died at Culloden.'

'Oh!' Their horror was mixed with fascination.

Christine began to enjoy shocking them. 'Lady Strathdallin works in the fields too. We hardly ever wear our shoes, and we both kilt up our petticoats to walk the blankets when we wash them. I hae to muck out the byre myself, sometimes.'

She saw Henrietta's little nose wrinkle fastidiously. 'Faugh! I dinna wonder your gown is so coarse. I'm amazed you havena brought the stink of the stable with you.'

Christine blushed, and angry tears sprang to her eyes. She knew that she had provoked their disgust, but the remark was far worse than she deserved.

'If the soldiers had burnt your home, maybe you'd hae to work in the fields yourselves!' she retorted. 'We've no time for music-lessons and fine dresses at Strathdallin. We're ower busy keeping ourselves alive.'

Elizabeth looked impressed, but Henrietta seemed to take the words as a challenge. 'You're only ages with us. You canna hae seen much of the looting in forty-six. You'd be only a bairn.'

'Yes, I did,' she answered. 'I dinna want to speak of it.'

'Go on,' mocked Henrietta. 'Tell us, we're not feared.'

She glared at them, dumb with misery. No words could make them feel it. They would never understand. The worst thing had happened when the English soldiers chased a stray Highlander across the bog. She had been out helping with the peats, and she had seen one of the soldiers blunder into the bright yellow-green moss. No one had been able to help him. She still had nightmares about it, and she felt sick now, remembering the look on his face as he was sucked down.

She came back from her horrible memories to find her two cousins staring at her with a startled expression. She put her hand up and found that tears were running down her cheeks. Henrietta went to the harpsichord and began to play. She kept looking up at Christine; she seemed to be sorry for what she had said.

'Can you sing, cousin?' she asked. Christine realized

that this was Henrietta's way of trying to bring the conversation back to a normal level. She smiled tremulously.

'Not in company, cousin. Whiles I sing to myself. Lilias has taught me some Gaelic songs.'

'What accomplishments do you hae?' asked Elizabeth.

'None.'

Once more they were dumbfounded.

'We,' said Henrietta, 'attend a school in the Canongate. We are boarders during the court vacations.'

'We are on holiday now,' explained Elizabeth. 'It is kept by the Honourable Mrs Erskine who is –' She stopped to poke Henrietta, and the two stood up to chant in chorus: 'Mistress of manners and decorum, wax-work, mould-work, silver landscapes, bugle-work, pastry-work and embroidery, music, principles of religion and loyalty, and tolerable good English.'

'Mama says we are sadly in need of the last,' sighed Henrietta on her own.

Christine laughed with them: Mrs Erskine's syllabus was evidently a long-standing joke with her pupils. The parties looked at each other with more friendliness, and in a few moments, Henrietta was encouraging Christine to join her sister in singing to her accompaniment on the harpsichord.

'Go on,' she urged. 'It's just a dreich old thing we're learning for Signor Rozzy, all about *crudele morte* and havers like yon – anyone can pick it up.'

They were in the middle of this when two boys entered the room with fishing-rods and creels.

'Geordie!' shrieked Henrietta as she rushed to the door. 'Mama said that you were to take your fish to the kitchen.'

Her cousins peered into Geordie's basket, while Christine hung back shyly. Geordie had plump, girlish cheeks, and was very like Elizabeth. She had already seen the dark boy who was with him. He had stepped out of the carriage beneath her window last night.

'You hae a visitor, Hetty,' said the dark boy.

Henrietta did not bother to look up from the basket. 'Och, it's a cousin of ours from the Highlands,' she said rudely. 'She bides up the stair in your grandmother's flat.' Christine's face burnt with hot waves of shame.

The boy put down his fishing-creel and made her a grave little bow. 'Miss Christine Murray,' he said, 'I am James Lindsay. This is my friend George Grant.'

Christine smiled at him gratefully, though her lips trembled. How odious Henrietta was! She forced herself to listen to the conversation and put on an air of gaiety. It was difficult to join in, because they were talking about people and events she knew nothing of. James Lindsay tried to talk to her, but Henrietta kept interrupting. She seemed to want all his attention.

'You've not cut your hair off, I see,' she said, looking critically at his smooth black curls.

'Did I say I would?'

'Och, yes, Jamie,' said Elizabeth. 'The last time you came to Mrs Erskine's dancing class. You said you couldna go into your third year at the College without a wig.'

'Aye, I mind on it now,' admitted Jamie cautiously.

'Was I there?' asked Geordie.

Henrietta put out the tip of her tongue. '*You* were at the billiard tables, like yon time you jouked your Greek classes.'

Geordie gasped and went pale. 'Hetty!'

'Dinna be feared,' she said scornfully. 'I'll not tell papa.' She turned back to Jamie. 'I wonder what colour wig you should wear, Jamie. A brown one, I think, and not ower much powder. It would be startling if you came out white, you being a dark man. Maybe you'll hae wee curls at the side, here.' She lifted her fingers laughingly to his hair.

Jamie gave her a hard look and removed the small white hand. 'You're a bold hizzie, Hetty Grant,' he said with mock-solemnity. 'I dinna ken what the laddies will do, when you're two-three years older.'

Once more he turned to Christine. 'My mother is anxious for your comfort. If there's anything amiss in the flat, you must tell us.'

'We are well-set,' Christine assured him. 'The linen is far more than we need for the three of us.'

He looked at her uncertainly. It was clear that although his thoughts were much kinder, he found her as strange as Henrietta did, and was not sure how to treat her.

Henrietta seized the situation.

'Jamie, such tales that Christine has been telling us! The folk up north live like savages.'

But Jamie refused to be diverted. He went on talking to Christine.

John Murray was silent and depressed when Christine met him again at the dinner-table. Balmuir did not press them to stay after the meal. Very unwillingly, Murray accepted their host's offer to send them home in his chaise. He thanked him stiffly, then recklessly gave a guinea to the footman who stood waiting for his drink-money from the departing guests. In the carriage, he seemed obsessed with his disappointment.

'Think of it,' he muttered, 'my own wife's cousin, and him only needing to put his pen to the paper. Then he offered me one of his daughter's old gowns for you, Christine! How dare he! Does he think we hae no pride?'

Christine choked back a sob. Even an old dress of Elizabeth's would have seemed new beside what she was wearing now.

'Will he not help you at all, father?'

Murray shrugged. 'Och, there was some clerk's post he offered me.'

She caught her breath in hope. 'What was that?'

'Balmuir has an interest in a clack of French and Dutch weavers just outside Edinburgh, at a place they call Little Picardy. The business is run by the managers of the Linen Company. Most of them canna speak English very well.

Balmuir wants me to take a hand with them, seeing I speak both French and Dutch, and help with the correspondence, forbye. The Company has many agents outside Edinburgh.'

Christine clenched her hands. 'Did you accept?'

'I didna downright refuse.' He sounded uncertain. Then he cleared his throat and frowned. 'Christine, my father aye said that a Highland gentleman could only do three things – drive cattle, go for a soldier, or keep an inn. Clerking isna gentleman's work.'

Christine could have shouted at him for his stupid pride. 'Did you say all yon to Balmuir?'

'I said I'd think it over. He's gien me letters for the master-weaver at Little Picardy, and one to Mr McCulloch of the Linen Company. I'm not going to use them, mind,' he blustered. He avoided her eyes.

Christine turned her face away. She loved her father, but more and more, she felt she could not admire the kind of person he was. He was full of hope one moment, full of despair the next. What kind of life would they have if he spent his time looking for insults, and brooding on his wrongs?

The carriage overtook George Grant and Jamie as they ran back to the burn. As they swept round the drive she could see all her companions at once: Jamie and George were waving their fishing-rods back at the house, where Henrietta and Elizabeth stood at the top of the steps and waved back.

Fierce jealousy swept over Christine. They had a fine life, those four young people! They wore silk and fine English cloth; their parents were important, respectable people. *She* had to be laughed at by their servants because her gown was tattered, and she was not even sure that next week she would have enough money to feed her family.

Then she looked at her father again. His face was tight and anxious, and he was twisting his fingers in and out of each other, so that she could see the marks on his wrists, though he did not know it. She could not bear to look at the scarred flesh.

Christine felt ashamed of herself. Maybe the terrible things that had happened had turned him into this kind of person. She tried to imagine what it was like to be imprisoned in the hulks; to drag out six years of exile; to come home and find no end to one's misfortune.

Once she had thought that no one could suffer more than the English soldier who drowned in the bog. Now she began to think that perhaps there were more dreadful things than a violent death; things that could twist a man's mind, and maim him worse than if he lost an arm or leg.

A wave of pity and tenderness came over her. She leaned forward and gently touched his sleeve, so that her fingertips rested on his wrist. 'Dinna fret, father. We'll manage.'

He jerked his head up, then looked at her bleakly. 'Aye, I suppose so.'

Christine sighed a little as she thought of the soft carpets and gilded mirrors at Balmuir House. Then she began planning how she could persuade her father to take the work that Lord Balmuir had offered him.

CHAPTER THREE

The Snuff-Box

CHRISTINE was wakened by the sound of the town guard scraping the garbage off the pavement with their shovels. The town had been busy long before, but she had slept heavily through the other noises.

Already Lilias had folded up her bed in the kitchen, and her father was sitting at the table, tapping a horn spoon against his plate. 'Quick, Lilias, I must be out of the house before St Giles strikes again.'

He looked embarrassed as Christine sat opposite him. 'I've decided to take this clerk's work,' he mumbled. 'Only for a wee while, mind, until I find something better.'

Christine drew a breath of relief. She rose again to find some bread and cheese for his dinner, and tied it in a napkin. Once he had broken the news, he seemed more cheerful. When he left he kissed her and whistled as he went down the stair.

After breakfast Christine settled the work of the house with Lilias and put her plaid over her shoulders. As she picked up a basket, the tirling-pin rasped on the door. Outside stood the water-carrier Jock Forbes. The barrel dripped down his back, and his leather shoulder-guard was green with damp.

'Will you hae a pennyworth the day, miss? I aye do my own land first.'

When he had filled their cistern, Christine went out to buy some meat and vegetables. On the landing she had to stand aside for a very old man, even older than Daddy Robertson. He wore a black silk suit and sparkling shoe-buckles, and looked very frail. A man dressed like a clerk

was helping him down the stair. Christine walked down
behind him.

'Canny does it, sir,' said the clerk as the old man fret-
fully tried to push him away.

Christine realized that he must be Lord Niddrie, the
elderly Lord of Session who lodged above. She heard more
about him later. He was eighty-nine, and although he had
long retired from the Bench he still imagined that he was
in office. Every day he went to Guffie's tavern, where the
landlord and customers let him sentence them and hang
them in mock-trials, several times a day. He lived alone
except for his clerk, who had turned himself into a man-
servant to look after his master in his dotage.

At the foot of the forestair Lord Niddrie stopped to pat
Jeanie the pig; the animal snuffed round his legs, then
trotted a few steps down the street behind him before returning to her sty.

'He aye has a word with Jeanie,' said Daddy Robertson.
'Poor soul, you hae to pity him. It's a gey sair thing to be
old and done.'

Christine stared in surprise. Daddy Robertson was not
much younger than Lord Niddrie, she thought. His wits
might be sharper, but he had to sit out in the cold piazza
and sell ribbons, while Lord Niddrie dressed like a man of
wealth. She puzzled over the incident many times afterwards.

Lucky the pie-woman came out to speak to her, and told
Christine where the markets were. Even so, it took her a
long time to find the stalls she was looking for, and it was
ten o'clock before she returned to the house.

There was a folded, unsealed letter on the parlour table,
and it was addressed in a spidery old hand to 'Miss Christine Murray'. Lilias said that the servant from downstairs
had brought it: it was from old Mrs Lindsay.

Inside, written with quaint formality, was an invitation
for Miss Christine Murray and her father to attend Mrs
Lindsay's 'four hours' which she held every second Thurs-

day afternoon. Lilias peered over Christine's shoulder.

'Is it not the strange thing,' she marvelled, 'for her to be at all this trouble of sending a letter, when she could hae said it in half a minute?'

Christine frowned reprovingly, though the same thought had come to her. 'When you live as throng as bees in a skep, Lilias, you hae to preserve the distinctions of rank and propriety,' she said grandly. She felt rather annoyed at the way Lilias' mouth twitched as she went back to the kitchen.

The formal invitation had a more homely P.S. attached.

'Your father tells me he kens one of the officers in the Castle, so I am sending word for him to come if he is disengaged. I should take it as a favour if you would come to me a wee while before the hour named above, so that we may become better acquaint. You will make certain, I hope, that your servant-lass takes her turn to clean down the stair before the Sabbath.'

Christine considered these three separate items with mixed feelings. Her father must have visited the Lindsays on his way out that morning. There was no other time he could have met them. She speculated for a time on what would happen when her father met Captain Binning; then her thoughts turned to the more urgent anxiety about Mrs Lindsay's request that she should present herself 'a wee while' before the other guests. How long was 'a wee while'? One hour, half an hour? She was tormented by doubt, and for the rest of the morning worried over the ordeal of presenting herself in polite Edinburgh society.

The maid opened the door at a quarter to four. She said that old Mrs Lindsay had slipped up the stair for a moment to give a dose of medicine to Jock Forbes's two children, who had fallen ill with colic. The house seemed strangely empty, considering that so many visitors were expected in fifteen minutes' time.

'The family's all out,' said the servant. 'The master's at John's Coffee-house with his writer, and young Mrs Lindsay's away to the circulating library.'

Christine looked about her, but could see no signs of preparation for the tea-party. She noticed that the room was very similar to the Murrays' parlour above it: there were the same painted wooden ceiling and the archway into the middle room, although the walls were wainscotted instead of showing the bare plaster. There was a bed in one corner, as well as the other furniture. Christine could not imagine where they all slept. She wondered if Jamie was still at Balmuir.

The seven-year-old girl entered and stared at Christine. 'I'm Sophia,' she announced at last. Before Christine could win her confidence there was a wailing from the back room. 'That's Robin,' said the little girl, and disappeared.

In a few moments, old Mrs Lindsay returned. She was even more intimidating at close quarters. She smoothed her dark silk as she subsided on to a chair, but she sat bolt upright without touching its back. Christine made an awkward curtsey and tried to thank her for the invitation.

'Come nearer, lassie, and let's hae a look at you. Hmphmn.' From a velvet side-pocket she took out a large snuff-box and gave herself a hearty pinch. 'You hae a bonny face, but you seem to have lost your tongue. Dinna be blate. Is your father coming?'

'I hae left a message with Lilias, madam,' stammered Christine. 'He'll cry in later, if he returns from his work in time.'

'Good. I'd be sorry for him to miss this billie of his from the Castle.' Her eyes narrowed shrewdly. 'I'm gey surprised to find your father so chief with an officer of King George.'

Christine stood tongue-tied, and her eyes fell on a pendant hanging by a black ribbon from the old woman's neck. The likeness she recognized at once, for Lady Strathdallin wore one much the same. Her eyes widened in amazement. Mrs Lindsay looked down, lifted the pendant up, and gazed at the portrait of Prince Charles. Her old lips twisted mischievously.

'Madam,' blurted Christine, 'is it not *treason* to wear such a thing?'

The old woman cackled with laughter. 'My, wait till I tell yon to my chums Lady Drymen and Miss Nimmo. They'll die laughing. All that's a long while past, my dear. Nobody cares a docken what a silly old body like me wears.'

Christine was shocked by Mrs Lindsay's frivolity, and came forward reluctantly as the skinny, ringed finger beckoned her nearer.

'Christine,' whispered Mrs Lindsay, her old eyes dancing, 'we females are sentimental creatures. I had it from the Prince himself when I went to his ball at Holyrood. But mind now, I'm not daft. I ken where my snuff comes from.' She took another enormous pinch and cackled again.

Christine was baffled. How could anyone make such a light matter of the cause for which her father had suffered so much? Mrs Lindsay gently pushed her towards the window with her ebony cane.

'No more of such dreich matters now. Go to the window and tell me if my guests are arriving.'

Christine looked down into the street. Several sedan-chairs clustered at the head of the close, and out of them emerged three or four old ladies, all gorgeously dressed, who moved in stately procession up the forestair. Lucky Robertson stood on the pavement and bobbed a curtsey to each one. Behind them came half a dozen men of assorted ages. They were powderéd, finely clad, with laced hats under their arms.

'Come away,' said Mrs Lindsay as the first tirl sounded at the door, 'we'll into my own room and greet them.'

Christine followed her into the room that lay directly under her father's, and was panelled in the same white-painted wood. There were a few chairs and a round lacquered table, but most of the space was taken up by an enormous curtained bed.

When the guests came in, six of them spread the skirts of their coats and sat on the bed with as much ceremony as if they had been shown into the music-room at Balmuir House. The other guests sat on the chairs and scarcely had room to stretch their legs.

Most of them spoke politely to Christine for a few moments, before they returned to their own conversations. She was confused by so many new names and faces; the chatter of so many voices in the small room made her head ache. Fortunately everyone was so crowded that her tattered gown was not conspicuous, and nobody could see how out of place she felt; but it was a relief when the silver tea-service appeared, and the maid handed round the tiny porcelain cups.

'You're Number Seven, I see,' rumbled a middle-aged voice beside her. The heavy-jowled man beside her pointed to the saucer, and Christine saw that her spoon had the figure '7' ornately engraved on the shank. Looking round, she saw that all the spoons were numbered.

'It's so as you can rax out for another cup, and no hae to drink another body's slops,' explained the man. 'Number Seven is gey chancy. I've never been here but Number Seven has broken a piece of china.'

Christine clung desperately to her saucer, feeling that she would rather die than draw attention to herself in this way.

The last to arrive was an officer in scarlet regimentals and a white wig. Christine disliked his supercilious manner, and hoped that if this were Captain Binning she would not have to talk to him before her father arrived. He did not look round for anyone when he came in, so she supposed that Mrs Lindsay had not yet told him the reason for his invitation.

The other Lindsays appeared for a short time. Old Mrs Lindsay whispered and pointed to her, and Jamie's parents

came over towards her. She liked their warm, friendly
faces, and began to feel less shy. After they left her, she
managed to keep up quite a spritely conversation with the
man beside her, who turned out to be a physician called
Dr Herries.

'Ah weel,' he said at last, 'I canna let my other ad-
mirers languish. Please to excuse me, Miss Murray.' He
stood up and lumbered cautiously over the tangle of legs
and petticoats. At once someone took his chair. It was
Jamie Lindsay.

'I thought I'd never win beside you,' he said. 'Yon Dr
Herries is an old blether.'

Christine brightened. 'I didna ken you were in Edinburgh.'

'I was at Balmuir for the day only. I hoped you'd be
here today.' He looked round the room and dropped his
voice. 'Does this not put you in mind of a coop of chickens?
Never mind, in a wee while Miss Menzies will favour us
with a song. Then they'll all sit down to whist in the
parlour.'

'I canna play whist,' said Christine in dismay.

'It doesna matter,' he reassured her. 'No more do I. Hae
you seen Henrietta?'

'No. Is my cousin in town?'

'Only for the day, with her father,' said Jamie. 'Balmuir
has a plea coming up with the General Assembly in May,
and he wants my father to speak for him. He's off to discuss
it with him now.'

'What kind of a plea?'

'A dispute over patronage. The living at Balmuir kirk
is vacant, and Balmuir and the other heritors want a
minister called McLure. He's passed his trials, but they'll
not accept him. He's a Moderate.'

'What's that?' asked Christine in bewilderment.

Jamie looked scandalized. 'He's a man of culture and
moderation who doesna threaten the folk sitting under
him with brimstone and sulphur. The kirk elders at Bal-

muir say his sermons are not sappy enough. They're High-
Fliers. They've rejected him, and the Presbytery support
the elders. So the Assembly is going to discipline the Presbytery for not inducting Mr McLure.' He glanced at Christine quickly. 'You dinna want to be wearied with all this
dull stuff.'

'Indeed, it is most diverting, Mr Lindsay,' she said
gravely.

Jamie looked puzzled, then burst out laughing as he
realized that she was teasing him. 'Forgie me, Christine.
When I leave the College I'm going to Leyden to study
law. Hetty says I'm as dreich as if I'd passed for an advocate already.'

For some reason she did not like this mention of Henrietta. 'Do you aye come to your grandmother's tea-parties?'
she asked.

'I usually cry in for a while. She likes to see me here, ever
since she first came to us from Pitcairnie.'

'Pitcairnie?'

Jamie began to talk about his family and the family
estate at Pitcairnie in Fife where his father's elder brother,
Robert, lived. The laird and his wife had no children, so
Jamie's sister Mary was being brought up by them. She
was the same age as Christine.

Old Mrs Lindsay had not stayed long at Pitcairnie after
her husband died. Jamie did not say why she had moved
to Edinburgh, but Christine guessed that the strong-
minded old woman would not relish having to give way
to a daughter-in-law. Nevertheless, the two families kept
in touch. Every week the carrier brought something from
the estate: a pair of pigeons, or apples, or jars of preserves.

Christine was enthralled by this information and went
on asking for more. Then suddenly she realized that for
the past half-hour she had done nothing but cross-question
Jamie about his family. He seemed to enjoy telling her,
but perhaps he was only being polite. She wondered if this
was the right way to behave at an Edinburgh tea-party.

Perhaps he thought her terribly rude, asking such familiar questions. She tried to think of another subject, then said more abruptly than she intended:

'Do you hae many winter amusements in Edinburgh?' She was proud of the remark.

To her horror, Jamie looked displeased. He paused. 'There is a dancing assembly, which I hae not yet attended. Then there are the music concerts, and we hae two theatres.' His voice became stiff and self-conscious. 'Mr Digges is considered very talented, and he has an excellent company. The College is all in raptures over the beautiful · Mrs Ward ... That puts me in mind of something. I must see if Henrietta has cried in. My mother wants the two lassies to join us at the play on December 3rd. Will you excuse me?'

He left her slowly, but Christine could see that he was annoyed. She was filled with misery as she realized what had happened. Jamie thought that she had changed the subject of their conversation because she was bored. How rude she must have seemed! Now she had offended him, and he would probably never talk to her again. There was no way to put the matter right. Christine thought bitterly to herself that Henrietta would have known just what to do. She would have made a joke of it, and shown that she had not really meant to be unkind.

She had almost decided to run after him to explain, when Mrs Lindsay tapped the floor with her stick.

'Miss Menzies is to gie us a song,' she announced. 'What's it to be, lassie?' Miss Menzies looked down and whispered modestly. 'Fine,' said Mrs Lindsay, 'that's a bonny lilting tune. Hold your wheesht, Davie man,' she said to a famous philosopher, 'and hear the lassie sing.'

Miss Menzies sang a sad Jacobite ballad about 'the wee white rose that grows across the sea.' It was sweet and plaintive, and drew a few sentimental tears from the ladies. It even affected the gentlemen, solid Whigs though most of them appeared to be. But it had nothing to do with the stink of the hulks at Tilbury, or her father's maimed wrists, or the English soldier dying horribly in the bog.

To Christine, deep in her private misery, it was unbearable. She began to hate all these sleek, self-confident people who made a game of feelings and loyalties they could not understand. She vowed that as soon as the song was over, she would leave them and stop her father from coming down. She could not endure the thought of his having to meet them.

But as soon as the song ended, the company rose without any other signal, and still applauding Miss Menzies, went to the other room to find their whist tables. Christine was left alone with one other person who had also been taken by surprise. It was Captain Binning. They looked at each other, caught in their mutual dilemma. It was impossible for either of them to leave the other alone in the room.

At last he sidled over with a look that showed he had no great hopes of her, but was prepared to do his social duty. Christine felt her hostility rise as he came nearer, but she managed to smile politely. She nerved herself for the conversation. If she was going to learn how to avoid blunders such as she had made with Jamie, she had better begin to practise now.

'You do not play whist, miss?' he asked, his eyes straying to the door.

'I've never taken a hand at cards, sir. Do you not play whist?'

He gave a short, barking laugh. 'Penny forfeits with old ladies are not my idea of an evening's play.' He took out his snuff-box, and eyed it doubtfully as if not sure whether to offer it to her. 'Strange habits you Scotch ladies have, but I suppose you have not begun yet.'

Christine hurriedly refused. At least he showed no interest in her, so it was easier to hide her dislike. Captain Binning tried to flick his snuff-box open, but the lid was stiff. He tried again and sent a shower of fine grains over Christine's lap. He jumped up in dismay.

'A thousand pardons, madam! The box was new this morning. I would not have had this happen for twenty guineas.' He flicked at Christine's gown with a lace handkerchief. The snuff flew up to her nose, and she sneezed twice. Captain Binning became even more agitated and flicked away as if her gown had been on fire.

They were in this situation when her father entered. He marched straight over.

'Captain Binning?'

The captain mistook his tone and retreated in embarrassment. 'Sir, you must not misunderstand. There was an accident with this cursed snuff-box.'

John Murray irritably waved the apology aside. 'Sir, I hae other business with you, if you will spare your time.'

Captain Binning bowed. 'Of course, sir, but I do not think I have the honour.'

Murray's face became grim. 'Is it so easy to forget your duties at Fort Augustus?'

The captain looked wary. 'That's a long time ago. So you were one of the insurgents against his Majesty?'

'I am John Murray of Tulmore.'

Captain Binning relaxed. Whatever he had feared, it was not this. 'I do not recall any gentleman of that name.'

Christine's father flushed, but his tone remained even. 'Sir, it doesna matter whether you remember or no. I hae no grievances to settle with *you*. I think you hae some information for me.'

'I?' Binning's eyebrows shot up almost to touch his white wig.

'I suppose you'll not mind the day I was brought to Fort Augustus. Four of us were captured about then. Another was called Ewan McDonnell – he was one of the four. Do you ken him?'

'Mr Murray, spare me the names. I knew of only the most notorious followers of the Prete – of the Chevalier.'

'Then,' said Murray harshly, 'here's the marrow of it in a word. I wasna let speak to my three friends who were taken before me. Either one of *them* told you where I was hiding, or someone they spoke to in the camp. I want to know the name of your informant.'

The captain, master of his snuff-box once more, slowly took a pinch. 'Why do you want to know this?'

Murray's eyes took on the wild glare that Christine had come to dread. 'I want to find the damnable wretch who took your money, and settle my score with him.'

'On my soul,' murmured Binning, 'I won't cant at you like a parson, but I'm almost glad I cannot tell you the poor fellow's name.'

Murray clenched his fists. 'You *must* remember. It isna possible you should forget.' He began to shout. 'There were gey few traitors in the Prince's army!'

Captain Binning began to back away. 'Sir, you must believe me. These incidents were so common – a vile campaign, I assure you, and so tedious. No wine to speak of, except your excellent French claret, of course, and the gaming had to be squeezed between two muster-duties – gaming! Why, devil take it,' he exclaimed, 'I *do* remember.' He stopped suddenly. 'Yes, but not the fellow's name, or even his face. One breechless Highlandman looked pretty like another to me.'

John Murray was too eager to take offence. He clutched the Captain's arm. 'Tell me what you remember.'

Christine hoped that the man was either dead or transported beyond her father's reach.

Captain Binning shook Murray off. 'Take your hand away, sir. I shall try to satisfy you. This fellow was brought to me, and we were going to shoot him out of hand, because he had wounded a sergeant. Then he said he knew where three other rebels were hiding, and would tell us if we spared his life.' He paused.

'Is that all?' demanded Murray in bitter disappointment.

Binning smiled as if he were enjoying himself. 'No. Look at this.' He brought out a snuff-box; not the plain brass container he had been using, but an elaborate affair of tortoiseshell mounted with silver. Inside embossed foliage and flowers were engraved the words:

'My heart is true. M.G. 1745.'

John Murray inspected every inch of it.

'Open it if you like,' said Binning. 'It is empty. The hinge is bent and I cannot use it any longer. Now, Mr Murray, I won this snuff-box from your traitor, as you call him, but I do *not* recollect his appearance, so it is no use questioning me further. I saw him when he was brought in, then again for half an hour on one rainy evening when I had nothing better to do. I do not even know when he left the camp. He had diced away all he had to my ensign, then on that night he lost this box to me. A pretty bauble, is it not? A pity it's no longer serviceable. It spoils the best mixture when the air comes in.'

Murray's fingers twisted covetously round the box. 'Will you sell it to me?'

'Will I *what*?' The soldier stared in contemptuous amazement, and his lips twisted. Pain for her father seared Christine.

'I would gie you five guineas,' pleaded John Murray.

'Oh, father,' whispered Christine, in shame.

Captain Binning tossed up his hand. 'Have it, my good sir. I had thought of giving it to my servant.' He bowed to Christine and went out.

It was eight o'clock. The whist-tables broke up, and the men retrieved their swords or canes. The paper lanterns of the servants bobbed up the stair as they came to fetch their mistresses. Some of the men obligingly went to summon sedan-chairs for the older ladies, and soon the soft Gaelic of the Highland porters echoed under the arcade. Lady Drymen leaned out of the back window and rang a silver hand-bell over the dark courtyard. In a moment, another lantern danced towards them, and a Negro boy in a scarlet turban came to escort her ten yards down the narrow wynd to her home. Miss Nimmo declined an invitation to make up an oyster party in a Cowgate cellar. Most of the men went off to sup at the taverns. Christine's head drooped as she followed her father up the turnpike stair; and John Murray held the tortoiseshell box pressed tightly in his hand like a jewel.

CHAPTER FOUR

Christine's Birthday

In November, the winter suddenly set in.

The weather did not become much colder at first but the crisp sunshine vanished, and there were days when thick clouds skimmed the mile-long jagged spine between castle and palace, and the east wind brought unceasing rain from the Firth.

John Murray was drenched every evening when he came home from work. Christine urged him to buy a great-coat. He refused for a week, then one day appeared in a coarse frieze garment which he shame-facedly said he had bought in a second-hand clothes shop in the High Street.

'It would be a waste to buy new cloth just to walk to Little Picardy,' he excused himself.

At first he spoke very little about his work. Some days he walked to Little Picardy and the weavers' cottages; on others he used to go to the offices of the Linen Company near Holyrood. He became friendly with the Company clerks, and sometimes went with them to their tavern in the evening. He was always back in time for supper, and never went out again after the meal. He seemed to avoid almost everyone, as if ashamed of his new life. Mr Lindsay once invited him to his club, the Greenshanks, that met every Wednesday in Guffie's tavern near the Mercat Cross. John Murray refused.

After supper he would put the snuff-box on the table and stare at it with his head in his hands. 'What can those initials mean, Christine? Whose name is it?'

'Och, father,' she would answer patiently for the twentieth time, 'there are a hundred names it could be – Guthrie, Gillespie, Gillanders!'

His obsession was like a banked furnace waiting to roar into flame. His everyday manner was cheerful; he had a joke for the pie-woman Lucky Robertson and the other tenants when he met them on the stair, yet whenever Christine hoped that he had stopped brooding on his sufferings, she would see that fierce, abstracted look in his eyes, and his hand would go to his coat-pocket, turning the snuff-box over and over.

The opening of the courts and university brought more activity to the streets, when the weather was good enough. The advocates clustered round the Mercat Cross with the merchants and caddies, or strolled in Parliament Close behind St Giles. Between eight and nine every morning Christine saw them walk over to the courts in their gowns, clutching their wigs and papers against the wind, as their clerks scurried behind them. Once she saw Lord Balmuir in procession with the other judges, in white and scarlet robes.

Lilias disliked bargaining with the market-women, so Christine usually shopped for their food. She had her favourite stalls in the Fleshmarket and Fishmarket, and began to enjoy the bustle and confusion of the street. Outside the Tron Church the kail-wives sold their vegetables; one of them was Lucky Robertson's sister, and when she found out where Christine lived she always kept back some of her best vegetables for her. She sold them cheaply, too; Christine supposed that the kail-wife must have heard how poor they were. She accepted the woman's kindness gratefully, but had the sense not to tell her father.

She soon knew all the tenants in Davidson's Land. The chimney-sweeps who shared the attics with Jock Forbes used to pull off their sooty hats when they met her on the stair; Lucky Robertson often ran out when she came back from shopping to press a hot pie into her hand. But the social distinctions were preserved: Mrs Lindsay might administer medicine or charity in an emergency, but apart from their encounters on the stair, each household kept strictly to itself.

There were disagreements too. One morning Christine came out and found Daddy Robertson sitting as usual under the piazza with his tray of pins and ribbons, but he was too occupied to speak to her. He shook with the silent laughter of the aged, showing his toothless gums, as he watched his daughter. Lucky straddled the pavement with her head thrown back and her hands aggressively planted on her hips. She was having a battle with some-one on the first floor.

'You're no supposed to toom your luggies afore ten o'clock,' she shouted.

'It *was* ten,' protested a quieter voice. 'The Town Guard were beating the drum up frae the Cross as I emptied the jugs.'

'They were not!' roared Lucky. 'You've done it afore, and I'll hae the law on you if you do it again. Just because you're ower genty to let folk see you at the window tipping out your nasties –'

The servant put her head indignantly out of the window.

'You girn if I tip them up the close, and you girn if I tip them in the street. Some folk canna be content.'

'You must do it at the proper time,' bellowed the pie-woman. 'You tipped them out afore the hour, and Jeanie here got an earful.'

'Och, yon pig!' said the servant scornfully.

Abruptly the dialogue ended. The head vanished so quickly that its owner must have been pulled inside. The window slammed down, and Lucky disappeared with a growl into her bakery.

Christine laughed and passed on. Her sympathies were with Lucky, because the Chisholms were the most un-friendly people on the stair. They kept very much to them-selves, and even the maid used to pass the other servants with her nose in the air.

The busiest part of the town was at the Mercat Cross where the caddies loitered for custom, and the merchants and advocates stood talking together. Towards mid-day, St Giles's bells played a medley of tunes and the crowd disappeared for its noon-time drink. Then they would come back and stand talking again until dinner-time.

Above the Mercat Cross were the Luckenbooths. Christine liked this part of the town best, and often found herself stopping in front of the shop windows when she knew she should have been hurrying home to help Lilias. She was torn between curiosity and shyness among the well-dressed women that thronged this part of the street. Hardly any of them wore tartan screens like her own. Lady Strathdallin had said that all women wore them in Edinburgh, silk or woollen according to their quality. The fashion must have changed since Lady Strathdallin's girlhood, for most of the women were wearing capes in gay colours, and straw hats tied under their chins.

The thought of her shabby clothes always depressed her. Her gown was now not only stained and old, but too thin for the November frost. She saved some money from her housekeeping allowance and from the same old-clothes shop where her father had bought his coat she brought home a tattered flannel petticoat. The man asked far too much for it; she bargained with him fiercely until he reduced it to fourpence. Then she carefully washed it and unpicked the pieces, to make a lining for her gown. She looked no better, but now at least she felt warm.

Every morning before she went out Christine saw Jamie wait at the foot of the stair for George Grant. Geordie would come up the street from the Canongate, and the two boys would walk to College Wynd together. Sometimes Jamie would have to wait ten minutes for his friend; Christine would press herself longingly against the glass and try to see what he read. The book always seemed very dull, but Jamie never looked up at the Murrays' windows.

Christine told herself that the Lindsays were very busy

these days, now that Mr Lindsay had pleas to make in the Court of Session and Jamie had gone back to his lectures at the College. It was stupid to feel neglected. She had only to tirl at the door downstairs to find young Mrs Lindsay and Sophia inside. Yet this seemed more difficult to do as the days went by.

She was beginning to lose hope that she would ever speak to Jamie again, when something happened. On Sundays Christine went with her father to the two services at St Giles. About a fortnight after Mrs Lindsay's tea-party, she looked up during one of the psalms in the morning service and saw the Lindsays.

She rebuked herself for letting her attention wander, but it became more and more tempting to look again. She struggled for a time; her face burnt and she felt the whole congregation was staring at her in stern reproof. Then she glanced up. She met Jamie's eyes, and he smiled. Christine smiled back; her heart lifted in a surge of relief and happiness.

The two families met outside after the service. Mr Lindsay asked them to take a stroll up the Castle Hill, and to Christine's delight, her father accepted. In the old days, said Mr Lindsay, the kirk elders used to patrol the streets between services to stop such ungodly practices; but people were becoming more liberal nowadays.

They walked with the crowd to the open ground between the end of the street and the huge bulk of the fortress, where small scarlet-coated figures dotted the walls, and the Union Jack fluttered on the highest point in Edinburgh. The ground was not very pleasant to walk on: it was unpaved and churned by the waggons that carried supplies to the garrison, but it was a favourite place with the citizens, and the grey sky had cleared for a few hours to give magnificent views to south and north.

'Do you play at the golf, Mr Murray?' asked Jamie's father.

'No, sir, I hae never learnt the game.'

'That's a gey pity. The Greenshanks hae a match to play against another club at Leith Links next month, and we're to be one man short.'

'It is my misfortune, Mr Lindsay.'

Christine walked ahead with Jamie. She was happy because he seemed to have forgotten their disagreement. They stood for a moment and looked at the view north: the Castle rock plunging into the marshy North Loch at their feet, the rough fields on the other side, and in the distance the blue glitter of the Firth and the hills of Fife.

'Is it ower windy for you here?' asked Jamie.

Christine held down her gown that whipped round her ankles and laughed with delight. 'I like it fine. The air's so clear and caller. How far can we see, Jamie?'

Jamie considered. 'You can see to the Lomonds and across the Tay on a fine day.'

'Could you see the Grampians from here?'

'I've never seen them myself.' He asked her suddenly: 'Christine, do you weary to be back at your old home?'

She strained her eyes towards the north, towards Strathdallin.

'Yes, yes, I do!' she cried fervently, then realized in the very moment of saying the words that they were not true. She glanced at her father. He was looking across the Firth and the longing was plain on his face. Christine wondered what had happened to her. She imagined herself back at Strathdallin with her father, or her father going back there without her. The result was the same. Something inside her had changed. She no longer felt homesick. She wanted to stay in Edinburgh, overcrowded, noisy and smelly though it was.

Jamie seemed disappointed at her answer. Christine pointed to the open ground beyond the North Loch. 'Jamie, why do the Edinburgh folk live cooped on this side of the loch? Why dinna they build their houses on the other side?'

'Many people would like to live there,' he said, 'and

there have been schemes to build along the Lang Dykes. But we hae to bide inside the line of the old city walls until there's an Act to extend the royalty of the city.' He looked at her ruefully. 'I mustn't weary you with these legal ploys, and bore you like I did at the tea-party.'

'But you didna bore me!' Christine cried, and in her agitation and eagerness to explain what had really happened, she caught hold of his hand. 'It was all a mistake. I was feared you'd think me too curious, and that's why I changed the subject.'

'And *I* was feared you thought me a boor, yon uncivil way I left you. Was it not daft of us both?'

They laughed together, then realized that their hands were still touching. Christine snatched hers away; there was an embarrassed silence, then Jamie hurried on: 'Well, then, would you like to bide over the loch in a fine new house?'

Christine bravely tried to match his light tone. 'Aye, I would. A house with big, light rooms and a stair to myself.'

'I can see it,' he teased her. 'Miss Christine Murray, the proud lassie who couldna bear the reek of the old town. All your suitors would catch their death of pneumonia as they struggled through the wind to court you!'

No doubt Henrietta could have managed a pretty reply. Christine was glad that her father came up just then, and Jamie could not see how he had made the blood mount in her cheeks.

After this Christine often went to the Lindsays' flat during the day. Young Mrs Lindsay was a quiet, gentle woman. When she spoke, it was usually to answer some question from her mother-in-law, who talked a great deal. Despite her age, old Mrs Lindsay was energetic and restless. She fretted when the weather kept her indoors, and after a few hours without any visitors she would summon a sedan-chair and 'go out a-jaunting', as she called it.

The house was very peaceful when there were only

young Mrs Lindsay and the children there. Mrs Lindsay sat sewing, and Sophia was as quiet as her mother. She spent most of the time dressing her doll. On the third occasion that Christine sat with them, she looked at the older girl shyly, then came forward and put the doll on her lap. Christine was very pleased by this gesture of friendship; she tried to help her, wishing that her fingers were more used to fine sewing. Mrs Lindsay watched them with her quiet smile.

'Shall I teach you to embroider, Christine?' she asked unexpectedly.

Christine brightened with pleasure. She did not think she would ever learn the tiny, elaborate stitches that grew so deftly under Mrs Lindsay's fingers; but for some time now she had longed for some skill that would take her away from the everyday drudgery of housekeeping. How pleasant it would be to be a young lady with at least one accomplishment!

'I'd like fine to learn,' she answered. She looked up at the painted ceiling. 'Could I embroider those birds and flowers up there? We have the same in our parlour. Then I'll have something to remind me when I leave Davidson's Land.'

Mrs Lindsay laughed. 'My dear lassie, you speak as if you're to vanish from us at any moment.'

Christine could have told her that this was exactly how she had felt for these last two weeks. It was a daft, senseless feeling that came over her sometimes, as if her life in the flat above the Lindsays was some fantastic dream.

'Besides,' went on Mrs Lindsay, 'to copy yon pattern would try the skill of the most expert seamstress. Yet, it's a pity, if you've set your heart on it. We'll try. Maybe one day you'll sew it on a waistcoat for some bonny gentleman.'

Mrs Lindsay sorted out her embroidery silks and they began the lesson. Christine was pleased to see her first clumsy efforts improve, although her fingers pricked for a long time afterwards. She must practise the stitches first, said Mrs Lindsay, and then they would draw the pattern.

In the evenings she sewed by candlelight after supper, though Lilias protested that she would ruin her eyes. When the jabs of the needle became unbearable she tried to copy the design from the rafters overhead, and borrowed pen and paper from her father.

'What are you doing, Christine?' he asked her one evening. 'Well,' he said, when she explained, 'dinna jig up and down yon way. You're casting a shadow on my book, and the print is hard enough already.'

She realized that the snuff-box was not on the table. It was the first evening it had not appeared. For a moment she forgot her embroidery. 'What are you reading, father?'

'Och, a dull Dutch volume on weaving linen. I borrowed it from Little Picardy.'

She looked at it when he left the room. It was full of diagrams of looms and thread patterns, and there were many pages of numerical tables. She could not understand the text; but she was pleased that her father was finding some interest in the work he had taken on so reluctantly.

He began bringing home other books of the same kind, which he said he had ordered from Ramsay's circulating library. Some of them were about growing and heckling flax and other matters that seemed to have very little to do with his work as a clerk. One was written by 'A Lover of His Country'. It was a treatise on the new methods of enclosure and fallowing. There was a paper slipped inside, on which John Murray had jotted down notes on raising quicksets and saplings for windbreaks.

He came in one day and found her reading this book. 'Are you setting up for a farmer, Christine?' he joked.

'Why are you reading all this? It surely canna be of service to you down at Broughton.'

He took the book from her. 'Balmuir has set me thinking, my dear. If we canna win back to Tulmore, there are other farms in Scotland, once I save the silver to take a lease. Maybe we'll emigrate. There's fine land out in America.'

He laughed at the expression on her face. 'Dinna be feared, it'll not happen tomorrow. It's only a thought I had. Surely you dinna want to stay in this city for the rest of your days?'

'I dinna ken what I want,' said Christine slowly.

John Murray pursed his lips as he looked at her. 'It's your mother you need now,' he said.

Christine did not understand him.

The next day was Christine's sixteenth birthday. Her father kissed her at breakfast and congratulated her, but did not give her a present. When he was in France, he had always sent Lady Strathdallin some money to buy her a gift, for her birthday. Christine was hurt, though she told herself that he was only being sensible, now they were so poor.

After he had left the house, Lilias came up to her with a small paper packet fastened with a pin. 'This is for your birthday, Miss Christine. You will ken it for something I had from Lady Strathdallin, but I've never used it.'

Inside was a yard of broad lace trimming. 'I have washed it every year in milk,' said Lilias, 'for it would be a shame to let it spoil.'

Christine was touched with her kindness, but when she tried to thank her, Lilias retreated behind a pile of dirty dishes, almost as distressed as if she had been rebuked.

While Christine was still looking at the lace, the tirling-ring was pulled loudly up and down, and when she went to open the door she saw not the water-carrier as she expected, but the young footman who had admitted her into Balmuir House. He looked very respectful now, as he handed over a large bundle wrapped in coarse cloth.

'Good morning, Miss Murray. Lord Balmuir told me to gie you this, and a letter with it.'

She took both from him and ran to the window-seat to

undo the parcel. Lilias looked on, exclaiming in Gaelic, as she unpacked three lengths of cloth: one woollen, one green linen, and another of blue French silk. There was a smaller length of white linen muslin.

Christine excitedly broke the seal of the letter.

Lord Balmuir wished his cousin a happy birthday, and hoped she would be so kind as to accept some linen from the looms on his estate and some muslin to make up a head-dress and ruffles to go with it. The silk and the woollen – well, they were odd lengths that his wife happened to come across as she was packing the muslin. He hoped she would approve of the colours. Young ladies were always perjink in such matters; his wife had chosen them, and she was reckoned to have tolerable good taste.

Christine stroked the fine cloth unbelievingly. How kind their cousin was! For one anxious moment she wondered if her father would be angry. Yet surely he could not be annoyed at such generosity.

There was an extra message on the back of the letter.

'The bearer has been instructed to take another letter to the Misses Chisholm who live in the first flat of Davidson's Land. If you will take the cloth to them, they will be pleased to make it up as you wish.'

Christine flushed with delight. 'Lilias, is this not a wonderful thing? I'll take it down straight away.'

As she wrapped the materials she tried to decide what style of gown she would order. The silk must be made into something grander than the plain round gown she was wearing now. A happy thought struck her, and she ran to fetch the doll that her father had given her. The fashion would suit her well, though it would have to be simplified. She would ask them to use Lilias's lace for the trimming. With the doll balanced on top of the heavy bale of cloth, she went to tirl at the dressmakers' door.

The Misses Chisholm were middle-aged women with fluttering hands, and soft, tremulous voices. They exclaimed in admiration over the materials; with deft, professional fingers they shook out the cloth and held it against Christine. Lord Balmuir's request was a very great honour, they said, and the doll's gown would be a bonny style to copy.

They cut out and pinned with amazing speed, but they protested that they had no special skill: they did a little fine sewing now and then, for a friend.

'A body can weary with nothing to do but go to tea-parties and concerts,' said the elder sister. 'Our dear mother aye said that a gentlewoman was none the worse for being able to sew her own gown.'

The room was piled high with half-finished garments and untrimmed straw hats. Christine was amused by their pretence, but sorry for them as well. Their own gowns were very worn and the apartment was poorly furnished.

When her father came home, she plunged at once into an account of what had happened. He stayed silent.

'Are you fashed with me, father?' she asked timidly.

He touched her arm. 'Not at all, Christine. I'm blyth for you to hae the new gowns. I wish I could hae bought them myself.'

'So you would, if we had the silver!' she said warmly. 'You canna help it.'

'There's one thing vexes me,' said John Murray. 'I wish he hadna sent the cloth today, or anyways, not before I'd seen you myself. Did you think I'd forget your birth-day?'

Christine was silent. Her father fetched a small leather box from his room. 'This was kept for you at Strathdallin, for a long while. I had it from the carrier today. They were your mother's. They're not much to speak about, but she wanted you to hae them.'

Inside the box were a necklace of coloured glass beads, and two silver rings. The rings were too large for her, but she flung her arms round him, distressed by her hard thoughts in the morning. 'They're bonny,' she cried, and was rewarded by his look of pleasure.

But he was upset because the rings did not fit her. 'We'll hae one of the goldsmiths in Parliament Close alter them. Let you and me go now – maybe there's one still open.'

Christine realized that he was anxious to make up for his apparent neglect, so she made ready to go with him, although it was dark and raining. They walked round the back of the Tolbooth and St Giles and found one jeweller who had not yet closed his shutters.

'You hae slim fingers,' he smiled at Christine. 'It'll hae to come in by quarter of an inch, this one. Not so much the other.' He held the ring up. 'A pretty wee thing. Yon Sandy Balfour of Perth was a fine craftsman. This would be one of his early pieces.'

John Murray stared. 'How do you ken all that?'

'Sir,' laughed the jeweller, 'I'd be a poor craftsman my-self if I didna ken the marks of my trade. See, yon's the Perth stamp, a lamb with a flag, and Sandy Balfour's initials, and a letter for the date. This would be made in thirty-five, would it no?'

'Aye, it was a gift to my wife the day after we were married.' A thoughtful look came on to his face, and with dismay, Christine realized what was going to happen. He took the tortoiseshell snuff-box out of his pocket.

'I'm anxious to trace the maker of this.'

The goldsmith screwed up his eyes as he inspected the silver mounting. 'The hinge is a wee thing ajee and hides the hall-mark ... aye, there it is. This is an Edinburgh piece, sir. There's the triple castle, and the letter for late forty-five to six. It must hae been made by David Patterson, for I ken no other maker here with those initials.'

'Is Mr Patterson still in business?'

'Aye, to the ruin of the rest of us!'

John Murray did not even smile at the joke. 'Where can I find him?' he asked.

The goldsmith walked to his door and pointed across the dark, empty square.

'Right across there, when it's daylight. But he's out of town today. He had to go to Linlithgow to bury his mother, poor old soul. He'll be back on Wednesday, maybe.'

'Thank you,' said John Murray. 'My daughter will come for the rings tomorrow.'

The rain swished gently on the flagstones of Parliament Close as they left the shop. John Murray walked as briskly as a young man.

'Christine,' he cried, 'what a dunder-headed fool I've been! The hall-mark – of course! Why didna I think of it for myself?'

Christine's heart was full of dread as they walked back to Davidson's Land.

CHAPTER FIVE

Riot

ON Tuesday, the third of December, the gowns were ready. The blue silk was Christine's favourite, but it seemed unlikely that she would ever have a chance to wear it. She folded it carefully away, and changed into the new green linen before going down to see young Mrs Lindsay.

Her embroidered birds and leaves had not turned out to be as elegant as she had hoped, but Mrs Lindsay praised her work and showed her two new stitches to use in the next part of her pattern.

The embroidery lesson was cut short when young Robin tripped over his petticoats and knocked his head on the table legs. Christine picked him up and distracted him until he stopped crying. She had never been interested in small children until she met Robin; there was something about his small, pugnacious face that appealed to her, and he now tottered to meet her every time she came into the house.

While they both fussed over the child, old Mrs Lindsay entered from her room. 'Is the terrible deed performed?' she asked, looking round as if she expected to see someone else there.

Her daughter-in-law handed Robin over to Christine. 'Dinna speak of it,' she said in a broken voice. 'I ken it has to be, but it breaks my heart.'

Old Mrs Lindsay snorted and took some snuff. 'You're soft, Peggy.'

The door was flung open, and in came Jamie with his father. Young Mrs Lindsay rose clasping her hands. Mr Lindsay pushed his son forward.

'Away in with you and show them all what a beau you look.'

Jamie stepped forward self-consciously. He was wearing a new brown wig, and Christine thought he looked very handsome.

'My, my,' said his grandmother ironically, 'the lassies will never keep their eyes off you tonight.'

Sophia ran in. She stared. 'Jamie, is it real?'

Jamie laughed. 'It's not my own hair, but it's a real wig.'

Sophia stretched up on tiptoe and cautiously touched a side-curl.

'Is your head *shaved* underneath?' she asked with wide eyes.

Young Mrs Lindsay shrieked and covered her face. Young Robin stretched up too and Christine leapt forward to stop him falling.

'Gie me, gie me!' shouted Robin. Jamie pulled off the wig and put it on Robin's head, and the child staggered round the room gurgling excitedly.

'Och, your head's not shaved at all,' said Sophia in disappointment. 'It's only cut short.'

Young Mrs Lindsay burst into tears. Her husband turned round in consternation. 'What ails you, Peggy, in Heaven's name?'

His mother chuckled. 'She's greeting because her bairn's a bairn no longer. It comes to us all, Peggy. He's a man now.'

'Aye,' said Mr Lindsay, 'he'll hae to come to the tavern with the Greenshanks, and sink his claret with the rest.'

His wife stopped crying; her gentle eyes flashed. 'Andrew Lindsay, you're not taking my laddie to any tavern with yon randy old Dr Herries and the rest of them. Dinna you think it!'

'I was joking,' protested the advocate.

'Mother,' said Jamie, 'the College hae their own tavern.' He added hastily: 'It's for the Debating Society, of course, and we only drink twopenny ale.'

Mrs Lindsay turned on her son, but before her wrath could fall there was another tirl at the door, and the maid showed in Henrietta. Jamie snatched the wig from Robin and put it back on his own head.

Henrietta greeted everyone by name, and gave Christine a cousinly kiss. She exclaimed over Jamie's wig but did not linger long on the subject, as she was anxious to tell them her own news.

'Is it not provoking,' she cried, 'here's Elizabeth canna come to the theatre tonight, nor myself either. Papa has been at our Canongate house this past week, and we were to hae followed him today with maid-servants and house-keeper.'

'But you *are* here, Hetty,' said Jamie.

She threw him a mournful glance. 'Aye, but only for the forenoon. Papa says I am to go back in the chaise after dinner.'

'Whatever's happened?' asked old Mrs Lindsay impatiently. 'Come, dinna spin it out, lassie.'

'Our housekeeper is ill, and Mama says she'll not move to Edinburgh without her. My father's been lodging at our Canongate house with only one man-servant, and he'll not allow Elizabeth and me to bide there without the women to attend us. Elizabeth is not so well herself, and I've come on my lone to the circulating library. So there's two seats in your box wasted. I'm gey vexed about it.'

They all exclaimed in sympathy, and Mrs Lindsay said how grieved she was that she could not offer Hetty a bed for the night. *That* would have solved everything: she could have gone back to Balmuir House in the morning. What a pity she had to miss the play!

Henrietta listened with downcast eyes, then turned with a look of speculation towards Christine. 'Cousin, isna this the most wearisome thing? Would it be possible – you canna be so throng up the stair – could I share *your* bed?'

Christine wanted to shout out 'No! No!' but she remained silent.

'Christine could come to the play instead of Elizabeth,' added Jamie quickly. Henrietta did not look pleased at this suggestion.

'Why, yes,' she said coolly. 'What a good idea.'

'Maybe your father would join us as well. There would be room,' said Mr Lindsay to Christine. They all looked at her.

Christine's thoughts span giddily. What an opportunity – yet what a price to pay. She made up her mind quickly. 'I'll hae to speak to my father,' she said. 'He's waiting on the Company clerk to gie him some letters for Little Picardy. Come up the stair with me, cousin, and we'll ask him.'

To her delight, her father accepted the invitation, saying that fortunately he would be home early today. Christine hoped that this response to the Lindsays' friendly advances showed a change in his general attitude: he had not talked about the snuff-box for nearly a week.

Henrietta asked Jamie to walk down the street with her 'to help me lift my bags from the chaise'. They returned with a suspiciously large amount of luggage, which Henrietta spread over Christine's bed.

'I brought all this,' she explained with obvious untruth, 'hoping to persuade Papa to let me stay with him in the Canongate.'

Christine clenched her hands angrily as she realized that Henrietta had planned all the time to stay with the Murrays.

'Christine, I'd hae greeted all night if I'd missed the play,' wheedled Henrietta. Then she darted out again, saying that she had promised to spend the afternoon with the Lindsays, and would come up to change her gown before they went to the theatre.

Christine tried to grapple with her dislike of her cousin. She was not helped by the sound of laughter on the stair, and the sight of Henrietta pulling Jamie along the street towards the booths round St Giles, no doubt to buy some sweetmeats. She gazed with fury at Henrietta's finery thrown casually across her bed.

Christine remembered how she had taken violent likes and dislikes to people when she was a child. Nowadays, she usually managed to like her acquaintances, or avoid them. The worst thing about it was that she did not feel a clean, open dislike of her cousin: her thoughts about her were petty and spiteful. She longed to humiliate her in front of the Lindsays.

Christine went to wash her face, hoping that the cold water would cool her mind as well.

Her father called her to him. 'Christine, the clerk has come with the letters, so I'll hae to be off.'

She helped him put on his great-coat. He stood smiling to himself for a moment.

'Henrietta's a taking wee thing,' he said. 'I mind on a lassie in Crieff, who had the same air. She'd toss her head at you and –' He broke off. 'That was before I met your mother.'

Christine said nothing, afraid of sounding spiteful. She wondered if Jamie found Henrietta as charming as her father did.

When Henrietta came to dress for the theatre she admired Christine's blue silk gown and said how well it suited her auburn hair. In fact, the gown was not nearly so fine as Henrietta's own; Christine said how kind Lady Balmuir had been to send the material, and Henrietta replied very pleasantly. But Henrietta on her own seemed to be a very different person from Henrietta in company.

Christine tried to think of some way to please her cousin.

'That's a bonny jewel you're wearing,' she said, admiring a gold clasp on Henrietta's gown.

'Mama gied it me for Christmas ... Dinna look so shocked, Christine! Mama is English. She aye gies us both a present at Christmas.'

Christine thought it best not to repeat what the minister of Strathdallin had said about the heathen custom of gift-giving on the twenty-fifth of December.

She helped dress her cousin's hair with a plume of coloured feathers that ought to have been ridiculous, but somehow managed to look delightful above her small, pert face. Then with linked arms they went down to the Lindsays' flat, and John Murray carried Henrietta's silk cloak over his arm.

'Lassies,' said Jamie as they entered, 'you look finer than the Countess of Eglinton and her seven bonny daughters.'

It was hard to tell which of them he admired more: he gave an arm to each as they walked down the street, and divided his conversation impartially between them.

Mr Lindsay had wanted to call sedan-chairs for his wife and the two girls. Mrs Lindsay would not hear of it. The rain had stopped and she wanted to see which of her friends were abroad that evening.

The play was *Hamlet*, and it was to be followed by a concert of songs and music. Jamie held forth learnedly about the works of Shakespeare as they walked down the street. Christine felt secretly triumphant when it appeared that she knew far more about the Prince of Denmark than Henrietta did.

When they arrived at the theatre, they found the mouth of the narrow wynd swarming with servants and sedan-porters. Out of two of the chairs came a couple of men in bands and dark clothing, who darted quickly out of sight.

'*Men*,' said Henrietta scornfully, 'using a chair. And they're young, forbye!'

'Aye,' smiled Mr Lindsay. 'The Reverend Mr Carlyle and his friend Mr Home. They're feared the Presbytery will suspend them if they're seen at the play.'

They pushed past the orange-sellers, and the hawkers who were doing a good trade with bottles of ale and porter. Ahead of them swaggered four young officers; Christine recognized one as the soldier who had travelled on the Leith coach with her father.

Mr Lindsay said something quickly over his shoulder to his wife. Christine thought this was about the officers, who were talking in loud, thick voices, and were not very steady on their feet.

They mounted to the box Mr Lindsay had engaged, and Christine gazed about her with delight. She had never been inside a theatre before. There had been dancing and throngs of gay people at Strathdallin before the Rising, but she hardly remembered them. This was her first taste of the fashionable pleasures of the city.

The house was packed, because it was Mrs Ward's benefit night; whatever the stricter officials of the church might say, most of Edinburgh society appeared to be there. Mr Lindsay pointed out some famous figures, and Christine glowed with excitement.

'You look very bonny tonight, my dear,' whispered Mrs Lindsay in her ear. 'Yon gentleman in the opposite box seems gey taken with you.'

Christine looked across and saw a young man who stood up and bowed in their direction. The bow was made to Mrs Lindsay, but his eyes were on Christine.

Mrs Lindsay laughed at her confusion. 'Dinna be fashed. It's only young Sandy Minto. I ken him well. He'll be round before the concert, no doubt, and I'll introduce him to you.'

'He's a coxcomb,' retorted Jamie ungraciously.

His mother turned round in surprise; but before she could speak a figure appeared in front of the curtain. There was an outbreak of shouting from the galleries where the servants attending their masters had free seats.

'One of the managers,' explained Mr Lindsay. 'I fear that one of the players must be ill. The gallery winna like that.'

The manager held up his hands imploringly, and at last made himself heard. 'We very much regret the indisposition of Mr Lee. Mr Wedderburn, a most accomplished young player, will undertake the part of King Claudius.'

There was more shouting from the galleries, and someone threw his hat across the pit. A candle was knocked down among the audience. There were indignant cries from the respectable citizens among whom it fell.

Mrs Lindsay turned anxiously to her husband. 'Andrew, did you not say that the managers had promised to keep the galleries in order this season? Are we safe?'

Jamie grinned. 'They'll not harm you, mother. The worthy bailies and tea-merchants in the pit will quell them.'

Henrietta pointed to the four officers, who sat close to the stage. 'That part of the audience seems as noisy as the galleries.' 'Well, well,' said Mr Lindsay soothingly, 'they'll hae to hold their wheesht once the play begins. Mr Digges and Mrs Ward are great favourites of the town, and they'll not let those young heroes spoil their pleasure.'

Jamie looked at Christine. 'Are you nervous?' he whispered.

'No.' She gave him an uncertain smile. She was glad when Mrs Ward appeared in front of the curtain to speak the prologue.

'Jamie,' mouthed Henrietta, 'I'm sure Shakespeare never wrote that.'

'Of course not,' he hissed back. 'Wheesht, Hetty.'

The curtain went up. Upon the battlements of Elsinore appeared the soldiers and the spectre. The soldiers were dressed like English grenadiers, and Hamlet wore a dishevelled neckcloth and periwig.

Christine glanced once or twice at her father as the tragedy of betrayal and vengeance unfolded. Then she became too absorbed in the play to look at anyone else in the box. *Hamlet* was not quite as she remembered it from her studies with Mr Nisbet. It was broken up by songs and musical items, and Mrs Ward as Queen Gertrude delivered an immensely long dying speech in heroic couplets.

The galleries behaved well during the play, except when Mr Wedderburn, the new actor, made his first appearance. When the curtain came down, they began to whistle and shout. Mr Lindsay assured his guests that they were only expressing their satisfaction, and there was no reason to be alarmed.

People began to visit each other's boxes, and Jamie glared across at Sandy Minto, as if daring him to come near them. The musicians stood up in their side-box, bowed to the audience, and began to play a selection of airs from *The Gentle Shepherd*.

The young officers were now sprawling with bottles in their hands. One of them walked towards the musicians' box, and told the orchestra to play something else. There was a murmur of displeasure from the pit, but the officer insisted, and the orchestra struck up with a tune from *The Beggars' Opera*.

Another of the soldiers, egged on by his friends, stumbled forward and stopped the music again. This time there were strong words of protest. Two middle-aged men left their places in the pit and went up to them. Christine recognized one of them as the man who had sat beside her at Mrs Lindsay's tea-party. She looked anxiously at young Mrs Lindsay, who seemed to be worried too, for she was tugging agitatedly at her husband's sleeve.

The argument below became hot; the middle-aged men returned to their seats, and the officer stretched up to the musicians' box.

'Give us a good tune,' he cried thickly, in a voice that clearly reached the other boxes. 'This is all Scotch airs too. Give us a march, you rebel cur. Give us *Culloden*.'

There were cries of outrage from the pit. The audience in the galleries realized that something was going on and leant over the railings. They hissed and shook their fists at the officers.

'Go back to London!' howled someone.

The officer who had called out scowled belligerently.

'Shame, shame, sir,' cried the pit with more restraint. 'Go back to your place at once.'

A few hats were thrown from the galleries, and struck the chandeliers, which began to sway dangerously, as people deliberately tried to hit them. Yelps from below showed that the hot grease was spilling from the candles. Hetty's mouth hung open with excitement, but Christine began to feel frightened. She had never been indoors with such a huge crowd before. Even when they had been quiet she had been oppressed by so many people hemming her in; now they were waving and shouting, and she was seized by panic. As some candles were knocked off a chandelier, she wondered fearfully what would happen if any fell against the curtain.

'Jamie,' she whispered in distress.

'Dinna be feared,' he answered quickly. 'If they dinna quit in a wee while, my father will see that you'll not come to harm.' He put an arm along the back of her chair, which reassured her a little; but still she felt stifled, and the walls seemed to be swaying to and fro in the heat.

The other three officers stood up to support their friend.

'*Culloden!*' they cried. 'Play the march *Culloden*!'

Directly below the Lindsays a man sprang on top of the benches and waved his hat. 'Are you standing for that, my countrymen?' he bellowed. 'Come on, Whigs though you be or no. Make them play *You're welcome Charles Stuart*!'

There was a roar of approval from the pit and the galleries whistled and cheered. The musicians put their heads together, and with frightened looks at the officers, began to play the Jacobite tune.

John Murray grasped the edge of the box and leaned over. 'I'll not believe it!' he cried incredulously. 'It's Ewan – Ewan McDonnell! He fought with me at Culloden. I must go down to him!'

Mr Lindsay put a hand on his arm. 'Sir, would that be

wise? There may be a riot at any moment, and I think it's time to take my wife and the lassies home.'

'You're right,' said John Murray reluctantly.

'Och, Mr Lindsay, just when it becomes exciting!' cried Henrietta.

'Dinna be so daft, Hetty,' said Jamie sternly. 'Shall I go in front, father?'

The theatre was now in uproar. The four officers had drawn their swords on the orchestra, and the musicians rushed out of the side-doors, hitting back at the soldiers with their violins. The soldiers leapt on the stage over the railings, and confronted the audience in martial attitudes, and with terrible threats. The most drunken of them fell flat on his face.

The anger of the audience turned to jeers and laughter. A storm of apple-cores, oranges, snuff-boxes, and even the broken-off ends of benches hurtled from the galleries towards the stage. The officers ran towards the back of the theatre, pushing the people in the pit aside.

'They're coming up the stairs!' yelled someone in the galleries. The audience in the pit and boxes began to jostle towards the doors, and Christine rose in terror.

'Please let's go!' she gasped.

'Come away,' said Jamie. 'My father and Mr Murray will take care of the others.' He gripped Christine's arm and almost pushed her down the stairs. When she looked back she saw Mr Lindsay pulling Henrietta away from the edge of the box. Her father waved her on.

Outside in the close they had to fight their way through a horde of Highland sedan-porters who were running towards the gallery entrance with their poles, intending to attack the officers from the rear. Jamie tried to protect Christine from the waving poles with his arms. She felt she would suffocate in the thick press of bodies. She closed her eyes and clung to him, not knowing where he was pulling her.

A man clutched Christine round the waist. Jamie

knocked him down, and the man sat in the gutter, looking surprised. As they reached the street, Christine gulped with relief, but she still clutched Jamie's arm for safety.

A line of paper lanterns and torches bobbed through the Netherbow Port, and they heard the beating of a drum as the Town Guard advanced on the riot. Windows were flung up all along the street, and a huge crowd collected at the mouth of the wynd. Jamie held Christine tightly until the others joined them.

'Thank Heaven!' cried Christine, and she ran to her father's side.

'A riot!' shouted Henrietta. 'Wait till I tell Elizabeth what she's missed.'

Mr Lindsay looked at her grimly. 'If those military imbeciles dinna lose hold of themselves completely, I daresay it'll end in nothing worse than a few bruises. I dinna ken what your father will say, Hetty.' He turned to his wife. 'I'm afraid you'll hae to walk, my dear. There's not a chairman in sight.'

Mrs Lindsay shuddered. 'I couldna bear one of the barbarians near me, Andrew. Let's away home the soonest possible.'

Back in Davidson's Land, Christine and Henrietta helped to unpin each other's gowns. Henrietta was effervescent; Christine had recovered from her fright, and had something else on her mind.

'It was terrible,' gloated Henrietta. 'They might hae killed us!' She climbed into bed beside her cousin.

'I dinna think so,' said Christine, with a yawn that turned into a shiver. 'Dowse the light, Hetty.'

Henrietta wriggled on to her elbows and played with the French doll. 'Not for a wee while,' she begged. 'I want to hae a crack with you.'

'Crack away,' said Christine resignedly, staring at the ceiling. She let Henrietta chatter on as she followed her own thoughts. Why had Jamie rushed out of the theatre with her in that way? His name caught her attention.

'Jamie seemed gey concerned about you. He didna hae a thought for the rest of us.' She sounded merely puzzled. 'What happened when you went outside?'

Christine's fingers slid to the sore place on her arm, and she remembered how Jamie had protected her against the drunken man. A thrill of pleasure went through her. 'Jamie knocked a man down in the close.'

'What for? Did he insult you?'

'Aye,' she said shortly. She wanted to keep the incident to herself. 'Hetty, snuff out the candle, please.'

Henrietta leaned over to do this, but her voice went on in the darkness. 'Christine, I wish *I* were old enough to be insulted. Not that I'd like it, of course, but it's fine to hae folk – well, looking at you, if you ken what I mean.'

Christine wondered what had happened to Sandy Minto who had looked at her across the theatre.

Henrietta's thoughts had moved on. 'Christine, do you ever think long to be married? *I* do. Mind, I wouldna take anyone with less than three thousand pounds a year.'

Christine laughed sleepily. 'Hetty, what clishmaclavers! You, a wee lassie, to be thinking about things like yon.'

'I'm near on fifteen,' protested Henrietta.

'What about Elizabeth?' asked Christine in amusement. 'Is it to be a duke for her?'

Henrietta took her remark seriously. 'Och, no. I think Elizabeth should marry Jamie.'

The words hit Christine like a blow out of the darkness. 'Jamie?' Her voice shook with viciousness. 'I aye thought you had a mind to him yourself.'

'Me?' said her cousin in a surprised voice. 'Och, no. I tease him whiles, and lead him on to – to –'

'To try your prentice hand?' Christine shouted furiously. The words went home.

'That was a gey unkind thing to say,' quavered Henrietta tearfully, and she began to cry. Christine listened to her in dismay. What on earth had made her say that to her cousin? She waited until the snivelling stopped. Then half in guilt, half in exasperation, she gave Henrietta a light poke.

'Hetty, I'm sorry. I hae an awful temper. Forgie me.'

'It doesna matter,' mumbled Henrietta, almost asleep. 'But I canna think –' she yawned – 'I canna think what made you blaze up yon way.'

CHAPTER SIX

The Goldsmith's Wife

NEXT morning Christine heard the water-carrier talking about the riot to Lucky Robertson. Fortunately it had ended without bloodshed. The mob had frog-marched the four officers to the Water Gate and there let them go, after ducking them a few times in the horse-pond.

'I doubt they didna much enjoy their walk back to the Castle,' ended Jock Forbes as he hitched up his barrel to continue his round.

Christine repeated what she had overheard to her father at breakfast. Then she asked him: 'Why did all those folk rise up in the pit last night when the officers called for *Culloden*? The galleries were a camsteerie lot, and they wanted a fight – but the merchants and bailies in the pit – surely they are all Whigs?'

Her father took a long draught of ale as he thought over his answer. 'Most of them have forgotten by now that they joined the Edinburgh Volunteers in forty-five to keep Prince Charles out of the city. I suppose they thought the officers had insulted their country.'

Christine remembered the Jacobite song at Mrs Lindsay's tea-party. 'Are they no longer feared of the Jacobites?'

Her father looked sad. 'All that steer is by now, Christine. The Prince will soon be only a name in a song.'

'Father, if we were now at Strathdallin and it was forty-five, would you do it again? Would you go out for the Prince?'

'Aye.'

'Even if you kent it would come to *this*?' she persisted. 'Why?'

Her father answered sharply: 'Because George of

Hanover is an usurper, and I couldna refuse to go when my chief called me out.' He went on more reflectively: 'Mind you, Christine, I dinna vex myself about it now. Our work is finished. The Jacobite cause is dead, and we must make the best of it with our German king.' His thoughts seemed to go back to the riot. 'That daft chiel Ewan McDonnell!' he exclaimed. 'He'll dance at the end of a rope one day.'

Christine mustered all her courage to ask him about something else. 'If you can be resigned to living under King George, why can you not put aside your private grievance as well?'

At once his face grew dark and angry. 'That's another thing altogether. I forbid you to question me about it, Christine. That puts me in mind of what I hae to do this forenoon. Put on your plaid, and we'll cry in on Mr Patterson the goldsmith before I walk down to the Company offices.'

'I'm weary of this snuff-box,' she answered rebelliously. 'Forbye, you dinna need me with you.'

He lifted her plaid from a chair and threw it at her. 'No odds, my lassie, you're coming. I'm your father; you'll do what I say, and never question the why or wherefore.'

'You dinna need me,' she repeated stubbornly. 'Hetty hasna risen yet, and she'll wonder where I've gone.'

'She can rise her lone,' retorted John Murray, 'and be off to her father's house without your help. Make haste, Christine.'

Christine kicked her feet into her shoes and threw the plaid round her shoulders. She jerked open the door and stamped down the turnpike stair without looking back at him. Her father followed, whistling rather loudly.

By the time they were walking down the street he had recovered from his fit of temper, and tried to chaff Christine out of her angry mood. She stayed obstinately silent.

'All right, my lady,' he said impatiently, 'take the dorts

if you will.' They remained very displeased with each other as they came into Parliament Close.

Mr Patterson was working at the bench with his apprentice and journeyman when they entered the shop, and his wife was sitting at the counter. As she rose slowly, Christine saw that she was expecting a child.

She smiled. 'I'll bring my husband to you, sir.' The precise chink-chink of the hammer stopped behind the partition, and Mr Patterson came back with his wife.

He gave a startled exclamation when John Murray put the snuff-box on the counter. 'How did you come by this, sir?'

John Murray eyed him suspiciously. 'You hae a good memory, Mr Patterson, to mind on a piece you made six years ago.'

'Well, well,' said the goldsmith, shaking his head in wry amusement.

John Murray leaned across the counter. 'I should like to hear the history of this box.'

'I canna tell you, sir,' said Mr Patterson.

'Why, is your order-book kept secret?'

The goldsmith turned to his wife. 'My dear, maybe you should go up the stair and rest yourself.' When she had gone, he added: 'My wife is to hae a bairn in the New Year. It's our first.'

'My felicitations to you both,' cried John Murray impatiently, 'but the history of the box is of the greatest importance to me. Who is "M.G."?'

'I canna tell you, sir.'

John Murray tried again. 'At least tell me for whom the box was intended, if you ken. It is some love-token, is it not? Who received it?'

'All right, I'll tell you,' Mr Patterson sighed. Christine found herself listening as eagerly as her father.

'In the winter of forty-five when the Chevalier occupied this town, a young lady came to me and asked me to make her a snuff-box.' He smiled. 'Like many another daft young lassie at the time, she'd lost her heart to one of the Prince's officers. She told me the whole story, because she wanted this inscription on the lid, and her papa didna approve – och, you ken how it is! Anyways, it all ended badly. She gied him the box, then the rascal jilted her, and marched out of the town. She never had a blink of him again. She came to me greeting, because she couldna pay for the box. Och, what a taking she was in! So I – but the rest doesna concern you,' he ended abruptly.

'What was the officer's name?'

'I never asked her.'

'Then I shall,' declared Murray. 'Does the young lady still bide in Edinburgh?'

There was a long silence. 'Sir, I canna tell you.'

'Why not, man, in Heaven's name?' There was anger and desperation in John Murray's voice, and his eyes had the glare that had made Captain Binning step back from him at the tea-party.

The goldsmith banged his hand on the counter. 'The young woman has since recovered from her disappointment. She has married well, and it would pain her to speak of these bygone ploys. Forbye, her husband wouldna like it.'

Christine saw her father hesitate, as his obsession struggled with his better nature. 'The lady's secret would be safe with me. I would never ask her name. I want only the name of the officer. Sir, I *must* ken it!'

'You will anger me,' warned Mr Patterson.

'I shall come again if you dinna tell me now.'

The goldsmith strode to the door of his shop. He was younger than John Murray and looked much stronger. 'Sir, go out of here before I think you no gentleman and summon the Town Guard.'

Murray's hand flew to his side; but he no longer wore a sword. There was nothing he could do. He left the shop, and Christine followed him, deeply ashamed, and not daring to look at Mr Patterson.

Her father walked slowly across the square. 'I canna bear to hae the worst of it!' he cried in vexation. 'It's such a little thing to tell me.'

'Yes, a little thing,' thought Christine, 'like Lord Balmuir signing the paper to gie him back Tulmore.' Her father could not see beyond his two obsessions. Her pity for him was swept away by irritation. He just could not see how people despised him when he behaved like this. Her thoughts must have risen to her face, for her father suddenly stopped in front of her.

'What are you looking so affronted for?' he demanded.

Christine twisted her fingers together. 'Father, how can you do it?' she burst out. 'Shaming us yon way! You made Mr Patterson think we had no manners or breeding at all. Yet you canna bear to let folk think how poor we are, as if that mattered!' She went on passionately: 'You didna hae the sense to buy yourself a great-coat, till I pushed you to it – and all because you couldna afford to buy it new! It's daft to be so proud.'

John Murray gripped her shoulders. 'Hae you finished yet?'

'Father, will you not see it?' cried Christine despairingly. 'You canna cast out with all the folk that winna do what you want.'

'Quite the wee philosopher, are you not?' he said sarcastically. But he did not try to quell her.

'Think a wee,' she begged him. 'Think how yon poor woman will feel to hae this thing cast up at her after so many years. Has she not had trauchle enough? How can you be so unkind?'

John Murray moved his feet restlessly, and stared around. He looked ashamed, but he covered it up by speaking roughly. 'Ach, you lassies are all the same. You think a broken heart's the end of the world.' He looked up at the clock. 'I'll hae to be off to Little Picardy. There's a new consignment of yarn in today, and I hae to check the invoices.'

'Father, please, will you stay away from that shop?'

'We'll see. I make no promises.' He tried to assert his authority, forgetting that she had to buy their food. 'Get you home, Christine. A young lassie shouldna be hanging round the streets.'

'Aye, father,' she said meekly. She watched him swagger off while she tried to remember what she had to buy. A figure slipped out from the shadow of St Giles's buttresses, and fell into step behind her father. There was no doubt that the man was following him. She recognized the caddy who had carried the chest on the first day she had met her father.

It was very strange; but she had been long enough in Edinburgh to know that the caddies made it their business to find out everything about anyone who lived in the town, or even visited it for a few days. She could not imagine what anyone would want to know about her father: apart from his obsession with the snuff-box, there was nothing in his present life that could possibly bring him into trouble. So she soon stopped worrying about this small mystery.

Jamie had left a message for her with Lilias.

'He was sore disappointed to miss you. He asked me twice was I sure you were not in the house.' Lilias' eyes twinkled in a way that made Christine feel very uncomfortable.

'What did he say?'

'He had a book for you, but he said he'd call again to gie it to you himself. He asked how you were after the riot last night. Then he said he had to help Miss Henrietta carry her bags down to her father's chaise.'

'But I didna see them as I walked back here,' said Christine.

'I think they were to cry in on Mrs Lindsay before they left. I expect they are still there.'

'Oh.' Christine felt exasperated. She wondered if she

would go down to find Jamie and Henrietta, then walk down the street with them. Something told her that she ought not to do this, but she did not know why. She tried to win support from Lilias. 'Maybe I could call in on the Lindsays myself.'

Lilias was wiping down the kitchen table. She said quietly: 'I wouldna be doing that if I were you, Miss Christine. You needna walk to the end of the glen to find him, so you can bide your time.'

Christine felt a hot flush begin at the back of her neck and spread over her face and breast, and every inch of her body. She felt both pleased and angry, and would have rushed from the room if Lilias had looked up. But Lilias followed her words with the everyday remark that they would soon be needing more coals: how much should she buy when the collier next came up their stair?

Lilias, at any rate, soon appeared to have forgotten the incident. Today they had to prepare a good dinner because John Murray was working in the Linen Company offices, and would take his meal at home. Usually the two of them made do with bread and cheese, or a pie bought from Lucky downstairs, in the middle of the day. While Lilias prepared the cock-a-leekie broth, and the skate, Christine went round the other three rooms to dust and sweep.

Towards dinner-time, there was a tirl at the door. Christine flew to it, joyfully certain that Jamie would be there. But it was Lord Balmuir.

'How's all with you, lassie?' he asked. 'Is your father home yet?'

Christine stood aside and tried to hide her disappointment. 'Sir, not yet. Will you please to come in and wait?'

'Aye, aye.' The old man limped in.

'Is your foot bad today?' she asked sympathetically. He grunted as he lowered himself into a chair.

'Och, whiles it is, and whiles it's not. But dinna call me "sir". I'm your cousin Adam. Here and gie me a kiss.'

Christine advanced her cheek cautiously, then said: 'I must thank you for your present, cousin Adam.'

He looked at her with satisfaction. 'That colour of green sets you well. I wish I had seen you in the silk. Hetty said you looked gey bonny.'

'Did she?' Christine could not control her surprise, and Lord Balmuir laughed. He took her hand. 'Christine, my wee daughter's not so bad as she's cried.'

'Oh, sir – I mean, cousin Adam, I hae never thought –' Christine floundered in embarrassment.

He swung her hand to and fro. 'Yes, you did, confess it. She's a wee minx when there's a laddie around, as well I ken. But she has a good heart, Christine. I'd like to see you friends.'

It was plain that he doted on Henrietta, and was prepared to talk about her for a long time. But he had hardly started when John Murray came in. Christine, who had dreaded meeting him after their quarrel, was glad that he was too busy with their guest to speak to her.

'I'll not keep you long from your dinner,' said Balmuir. 'There's a wee matter I wish to discuss with you.'

'Surely you'll stay and hae your meal with us,' said Murray. Christine was pleased to see how friendly and at his ease with Balmuir he now seemed.

'No, I thank you,' said Balmuir. 'I am promised to Henrietta. I must pack the wench into the chaise myself after dinner, for she might make some excuse to bide on, if I dinna send her home to her mother this afternoon. She's wearying to be back in town for the winter.'

'Well, Balmuir, what is this matter?'

Christine started to leave the room, but Balmuir told her to take no notice of him, but carry on with her household tasks.

'John, I want your help. I have a scheme to increase the production of flax and linen yarn in the Highlands. McCulloch thinks it's a chancy affair, and is not that keen to try it.'

John Murray raised his hand. 'Sir, I canna go behind my employers, if they dinna –'

'Nothing of the sort,' interrupted Balmuir. 'They ken I'm to speak to you, but it's a wee thing kittle to do it in the Company offices.'

John Murray smiled. 'Me being a junior clerk. Of course, it wouldna do at all,' he joked.

Christine listened in surprise. This indeed was a new tone for her father! He certainly had changed over the past few weeks, she thought.

'Here's my idea,' said Balmuir. 'I want the weavers at Little Picardy to order their supplies of yarn from Perthshire, or further north.'

'Surely it is more convenient to hae it from the local fields, or from Fife, as they do now?' said John Murray.

'Aye, but if the northern growers of flax had to answer a greater demand, then more would be grown in the north. Already we hae agents in Cromarty and other places, as you ken, whom we put there to encourage the local growth. But that's all to be spun locally. Now, if they hae to answer orders from a distance – when they canna say "My dear Donald, you will have to be waiting, for herself does not feel inclined to harvest the flax this year" – well, they'll hae to be more businesslike, will they not?'

'Sir,' laughed John Murray, 'you dinna hae a great opinion of our Highland persistence.'

'Not at all, John man. It's the same with my own folk at Balmuir. Do you think my scheme would answer?'

'It might answer very well,' said Murray slowly. 'But what way do you need my help?'

'I would like to try my scheme out by making a link between Little Picardy and farmers in Perthshire. Then we'll extend it to other centres, if it succeeds. In the end we shall return to using local supplies, once we hae stimulated all the growth of flax we need. *You* can tell us where best in Perthshire we could place our orders.'

Murray nodded his head. 'I'm not a flax-farmer, but I

think I could do that. I ken the district well, and what ground's the best to grow flax.'

'Exactly,' said Balmuir. 'Here, look at this.' He spread a map on the table. 'I've marked a few likely places, but I want your opinion – where we could grow the flax, where we could set up the spinning-schools.'

The discussion went on for some time. Christine was in the kitchen when Lord Balmuir came to say goodbye to her.

'I'll be seeing more of you,' he said affectionately. 'And mind on what I said about Henrietta.'

When they were having supper that evening, John Murray suddenly laid down his spoon and said: 'I had an uncanny feeling as I came up the street tonight.' He stopped and looked at her uncertainly. Christine remembered how he had always laughed at the wonderful tales of second-sight and magic that the crofters told each other at Strathdallin. 'I thought someone followed me, all the way,' he went on. 'But every time I looked back, there was no one there.'

'It would be gey mirk,' she pointed out. 'You wouldna see.'

'Aye, but –' He rose slowly to his feet. 'There's someone outside our door.'

'It's the common stair, father!'

'They're standing there, Christine.' He went to the door and quickly pulled it open. A woman stood outside with upraised hand, as if she had been about to tirl. She was muffled in a large plaid which covered her face.

'Who are you?' demanded John Murray harshly. 'What do you want?' He pulled her into the light of the room. She drew the plaid from her face, and they saw that she was the goldsmith's wife.

'Mrs Patterson!' exclaimed Murray.

'Sir, forgie me. I had a caddy follow you to discover your name and lodging. I hae been waiting on you to come home.' She was shivering with cold. Christine pulled over a chair, and made her sit down. The woman murmured, 'Thank you, lassie,' but her eyes stayed fixed desperately on John Murray.

'Mrs Patterson, this is very strange,' he said.

'Sir, I had to see you.' Her voice rose. 'You hae sorely angered my husband. I beg you, dinna come back to his shop.'

There was a long silence in the room. Murray looked very ill at ease. 'Madam, my business with your husband isna settled.'

Mrs Patterson clasped her hands. 'Canna you tell why he's so sweer to tell you?'

John Murray shifted from one foot to the other. 'A too nice sense of obligation towards his customers, I suppose.'

'Na, na. Before I was married, my name was Mary Gilchrist. Mr Murray, *I* am the woman who ordered the snuff-box.'

'You!' cried Murray in astonishment, and Christine gasped with him.

Mrs Patterson put her hands to her face. 'I was a heedless lassie at the time. My husband canna bear to hae it cast up by my mother or the neighbours. Please, please, leave us alone, for he canna help you, and I've told you all I hae to tell.' Her voice broke.

John Murray seized her wrists. 'Not *all*, madam. The name – tell me the name of your friend.'

She pulled herself away. 'No. You mean to harm him, do you not? I saw it in your face this forenoon.'

John Murray was silent for a while, then he said: 'Madam, he did me a great wrong. I hae a right to revenge.'

The woman looked at Christine, as if seeking her help. Then she leant back wearily. 'No greater wrong than he did to me. Can you not forgie him, too?'

'Do you still love the fellow?' asked Murray.

'No,' she said in a low voice.

'Then it should please you to see him get what he deserves.'

'No!' she cried vehemently.

Christine pulled at her father's arm. But there was no need. He sighed and took the snuff-box out of his pocket. 'I'll not ask you again, madam. This box is no use to me now. Would you like it?'

The woman held it to the light and turned it over, stroking the embossed silver with a curious gesture. 'How did it come to you?'

'He lost it at dice to an English officer, who gave it to me.'

'I wonder he kept it so long,' she said bitterly. 'He would hae gamed away his soul, if he could. Yet he was so pleased when I gied it to him.' Her gaze softened, and she seemed to be talking to herself. 'He was aye so perjink about his snuff. The mixture had to be just so, and it had to be sifted.' She laughed. 'Aye and on he'd bring out this wee sifting spoon, even to take the merest pinch. It was silver set with one garnet. A bonny wee thing. I had the box made to match it . . .'

Her voice died, and suddenly she realized where she was. 'Och, what does it matter now? I must be away home.'

Christine touched her arm. 'Dinna distress yourself. You'll not hear of this again.'

John Murray bowed. 'Be assured, madam, I shall not come to your husband's shop.'

Mrs Patterson put the snuff-box on the table. 'Maybe it's best you should keep it. I dinna think on him at all now, but it's best not to be reminded.' Again she touched it with the strange, caressing gesture, then pulled her hand away as if the metal had burnt her. She refused Murray's offer to light her down the stair, and went away without saying goodbye.

After she left, Christine took her father's hand. 'I'm glad you didna press her.'

'Poor woman,' said John Murray compassionately. 'You

were right, Christine. It wouldna hae done to go back and fash the poor soul.'

Christine was thinking about the look on Mrs Patterson's face as she held the snuff-box. 'Does she still love him, father?'

John Murray laughed at her. 'Aye and no. She loves him when she thinks about it.'

'That's ower hard for me,' she complained. 'I dinna understand.'

He patted her shoulder. 'You will, my lassie, you will.'

Christine began to clear away the supper dishes. 'That's an end of it,' she said thankfully. 'You ken who she was, and you canna do more.'

John Murray brought the Bible from his room for their evening prayers. 'I wouldna say that, Christine,' he answered gravely. 'I canna question Mrs Patterson again, but there are others who can tell me what I want to know. I can find out her family, and whom she spent her time with, yon winter of forty-five. There are a hundred ways to do it – she need never ken at all.'

Christine realized that however her father might have changed in other ways, in this one obsession he remained the same. She shrugged wearily. 'Such a time it will take, father!'

'I hae time enough, Christine. All the rest of my days.'

CHAPTER SEVEN

Ewan McDonnell

WHEN Christine rose next morning, she found that Lord Balmuir's map was spread on the parlour table. Her father must have worked late on it after she went to sleep, for the rushlight beside it had burnt to nothing in its holder. She read the names of places she knew, and in large red letters: STRATHDALLIN.

Her father came up behind her. 'I've been working hard,' he said. 'I hope Balmuir will be pleased.'

'Is the whole of Strathdallin to go for flax?' she asked.

'Na, na, it wouldna be suitable. But they could grow it at Tulmore, and run a heckling mill off the river.'

Christine traced the course of the Dallin with her finger. 'Then it doesna grieve you, father?'

He put a hand on her shoulder. 'Aye, it grieves me, but I hae learnt to thole it. I'll save my wages, and we'll lease a farm. Not as tacksman this time – we'll hae to work the land ourselves.' He looked at her hard. 'Christine, we quarrelled yesterday.'

She hung her head. 'Aye.'

'You're not a bairn now, my dear. We must learn to differ. There are matters you must not meddle with. And maybe I hae to learn that you can be right, and I wrong.'

'I think I ken what you mean,' she said in a low voice.

'Fine, then.' He went to fetch his great-coat, and when he had put it on, held up his arm to look at the huge, buttoned cuff. 'I was sweer to wear another body's old clouts at first, but now I'm glad of its warmth. It's good cloth, is it not?' The question was anxiously put.

'It's the finest English cloth,' she said warmly. 'Whoever had it first was gey feckless to let it go.'

93

He seemed relieved. 'Aye, that's what I thought.' As he went out, he said: 'I'd be obliged if you'd leave the map where it is. I want to work on it tonight.'

Christine thought with pleasure about the way her father had changed in the past month. Perhaps the snuff-box and all the horrible memories that went with it would gradually be forgotten.

As she helped Lilias wash the breakfast dishes, she could not understand why she felt so miserable. Then she remembered: Jamie had not called in yesterday as he had promised.

She went to the parlour windows, hoping to see him wait for George Grant. She did not like to stand there too long, after Lilias' remark yesterday, so in the end she missed him.

Christine did the shopping that morning in a mood of discontentment. Usually, when she was bored or depressed, she would go to the Krames, the small booths squeezed between the Luckenbooths and the southern buttresses of St Giles. She enjoyed watching the stall-holders cajole people into buying the goods that she could never afford herself. There was even a troupe of performing dogs here, that used to mince along on their hind legs with frills round their necks, dancing in front of a man playing a flute.

Today, all this had no appeal. She felt even more depressed when she saw a notice pasted on a board, concerning the riot in the Canongate theatre. It reminded her too much of the cause of her dissatisfaction.

For the future, the notice declared, *the Band of Music is not to play any Tunes at the desire of the Audience, but select pieces appointed by the Managers.*

When Christine returned home, she heard Gaelic being spoken in the kitchen, interrupted by bursts of laughter. With Lilias was the man whom her father had recognized in the theatre.

'Miss Christine, here is your father's friend!' cried

Lilias. She was bright-eyed, and had the air of a woman who had been much flattered. Christine noticed with astonishment, and for the first time, that Lilias was still young, and her face was very pretty when it opened with laughter.

The man stood with one foot on a chair. His whole body gave an impression of thickness; his legs, his short neck, his blunt fingers, even his nose and lips – all seemed too coarse and solid. The strangest thing about him was his hair, or perhaps his wig, for she could not tell if he wore one. It frizzled in tight brown curls all the way to his pig-tail, and was as thick and lustreless as a lamb's fleece. His pock-marked face was ugly; yet he had an attractive, almost aggressive vitality, that Christine would not have noticed a few months ago. She could not put a name to it, but she knew it was this that had caused the change in Lilias, and she shrank back as she felt the man's attention turn to her.

'So you are John's daughter,' he said, staring at her. His voice was husky, neither Scots nor English. The intonation seemed to belong to another language.

He moved across the room, and an unreasonable panic swept through her. But he had come only to lift his hat from the table.

She tried to meet his gaze. 'My father is not at home, sir.'

'So this young woman tells me, my dear. I hear that my old friend is no longer a gentleman, but has turned himself into a clerk.' His small black eyes screwed up in mockery, as if he were trying to provoke her. Christine tried not to show her discomfort.

'My father works for the British Linen Company,' she said coldly. 'We had no money after Strathdallin was confiscated.'

He tossed up his laced hat and caught it. 'What a pity that such a pretty young lass should be deprived, all for her father's folly!' The tone was ironic, but it was shading into flattery. Christine began to understand how he had worked on Lilias.

'My father thought you were foolish yourself, at the play!' she thrust back.

He threw back his curly head and laughed. 'So you were in the theatre, were you? It irks me to see so many fat fellows sit still when Prince Charles is insulted. I am in the Prince's service, my dear. I am sorry your father has so tamely given up our cause. I must put some mettle into him. The Prince needs good men for his service. When does your father come home?'

'Sometimes early, sometimes late, but never later than half-past eight.' How incredibly rash he was, she thought. How did he dare to speak about his business so openly?

'Good.' Ewan put on his hat and picked up his cane. 'I shall return at that hour. Goodbye, ma jolie,' he said to Lilias. 'I look forward to our next meeting.' He seized her loosely by the waist and kissed her. Lilias giggled and glanced impudently at Christine. Ewan walked to the door and bowed. 'Goodbye, Miss Murray. Pray do not trouble to see me out.'

Christine did not answer. She shut the kitchen door behind him, and put her back against it. Her eyes flashed. She could not allow Lilias to think that she had noticed nothing, or was too timid to rebuke her.

'Lilias,' she said sternly, and forced the servant to meet her eyes. But all the vitality had gone out of Lilias, once Ewan left the kitchen. She stood there, meek and silent, as if the last half-hour had never existed. Christine was glad she did not have to use the words that had been on her tongue. She opened the shopping-basket instead.

'Lilias,' she said, 'will you please pluck and draw this fowl?'

All day Christine wondered about what effect Ewan McDonnell might have on her father. He was a reckless man, she thought. He would not care how much harm he did to her father, so long as it brought him what he wanted.

'He'll dance at the end of a rope one day,' John Murray had said. Ewan seemed to be working for the Jacobites, and it sounded as if he intended to persuade her father to join him. She had no idea what the work would be; but it would be treasonable, and the punishment for treason was death. She must warn her father before Ewan met him. Even if he did not do what Ewan wanted, he might thoughtlessly encourage him to come about the house, and then people would think that he, too, was working for the Jacobites.

She wondered how she could warn her father. He would be very displeased if she interrupted his work at Little Picardy, and besides, she might be overheard. The best thing would be to catch him before he came home, if he stayed at work late. If she could meet him at the Nether-bow Port, that would be time enough.

The afternoon became very cold; lowering clouds brought darkness by half-past four. She decided to wait until nearly eight o'clock before she left the house. Even then, she might have a long wait, but that would be better than the risk that Ewan might come to the house before she left.

The street looked very black outside at quarter to eight, and the coal-fire in the parlour was hard to leave. As Christine went out on the landing, a light wavered round the bend of the turnpike stair. It was Jamie holding a candle. There was a book in his other hand.

'I've brought the Shakespeare you wanted to borrow.' He handed over the thick leather-bound volume.

'Dinna go away,' said Christine. 'I'll just put this inby.' She ran in with the book and came back to him.

'I'm sorry I couldna come yesterday,' said Jamie, 'but you were out in the forenoon, and in the evening –' he laughed rather awkwardly – 'my father took me to a meeting of the Greenshanks.'

'Oh.' Christine thought dismally of the convivial, masculine world that Jamie had now entered, and wondered if she would see even less of him. 'So your mother –' She broke off. Perhaps it would be tactless to remind him that his mother still looked on him as a young boy.

'I was early away,' he assured her. 'My father doesna really want me at his club every Wednesday. When I pass for an advocate, I'll hae my own. Geordie and I will form a new one. We're going to call it "The Cock-a-leekie Club." We'll hae none in it but Collegers of our own year.'

Despite the freezing air of the landing, he was all set to tell her about the proceedings and rules of the projected society, but the sound of St Giles's bell reminded Christine that her father would soon be walking up the street.

'I'm sorry, Jamie, I hae to go.'

'You're never going outside!' he said, looking at her plaid.

'Aye, I hae to take a message. I'm going to meet my father at the Netherbow Port.'

Jamie looked agitated. 'Could you not hae a caddy take it, or send the servant-lassie in your place?'

'I dinna see why Lilias should take the cold instead of me,' she replied tartly.

'It's not the cold I'm thinking on, Christine. It's not right for you to walk down the street your lone.'

Her nerves were already strained by anxiety for her father, and Jamie's caution vexed her. She was also unreasonably annoyed that he had not called in yesterday.

'Why not? I do it every day of my life when I go to the markets.'

'It's not the same at night,' said Jamie unhappily.

'Why?' jeered Christine. 'What are you feared will happen to me?'

'Och, nothing,' he answered with irritation. 'I daresay not a soul would speak to you between here and the Port of Leith. But maybe they would. It's not the thing for a young lady to be seen out alone in the street at night. Christine, *you're not to go!*'

'Who's to hinder me, Jamie Lindsay?' She wound the plaid tightly round her shoulders and pushed past him. Jamie glowered in silence. Looking back over the candle-flame, Christine had a strange pang of annoyance: not because he was so cautious, but because he was only a half-grown boy, and she knew he could not stop her. She felt an urge to goad him further.

'If you're in such a taking about me,' she flung over her shoulder, 'why do you not come down the street with me yourself?'

'Christine!' The candle nearly fell out of his hand. 'I couldna. What would folk think about you if they saw us?'

She came back up the stair. 'Well,' she mocked. 'What would they think?'

The conversation suddenly came to a standstill. Christine's bravado ebbed, and she saw Jamie's anger at her pertness change to a look of perplexity, followed by something too complicated for her to understand. He stepped forward, and it reminded her of Ewan coming towards her in the kitchen. They stared at each other without speaking, until Christine felt that something inside her was going to burst into stars like a rocket.

Then the candle spluttered, and a drop of hot grease fell on her hand. She cried out, and put her burnt finger in her mouth. Jamie apologized, and in the confusion of the small accident, everything became normal again.

'Well, I see I canna stop you,' he said with resignation. 'But, Christine, mind, dinna speak to anyone in the street.'

'Dinna fash yourself!' she laughed back at him. 'I won't!'

Only a few gleams of light were thrown into the street, from unshuttered windows and open doorways. Jeanie the pig was grunting to herself as she rooted in the gutter, and Christine almost tripped over her. A few shops were still open, and raucous shouts and bursts of song came from the taverns. But there were not many people on the street. She had to cross from one side to the other, to avoid the men who lurched out of the ale-houses and groped along the wall.

Something brushed her cheek over and over again; myriads of tiny snowflakes were drifting through the squares of light above her head. As she passed the Tolbooth, she heard footsteps approaching her. She was too frightened to walk under the prison walls, but the street here was so narrow that it was impossible to avoid the person coming towards her. Between them, a shaft of light streamed from the head of a close. She slowed her steps, but misjudged the distance, and the light fell on her first.

Christine stood still. Nothing on earth could have made her step from her island of light into the darkness.

'There now, my pretty lass,' said a hoarse voice, 'what will your plea be?' A hand came out of the gloom and touched her. Christine was about to scream and run away when the man stepped into the light, and she recognized the old judge, Lord Niddrie.

He clutched her hand, and tilted his head to one side. 'It's no good,' he said mournfully. 'I canna help you. The man has to die, dear lassie. It's a clear case of treason. Hang him and draw him, and quarter him while the body's still alive. That's the law.'

More footsteps pounded up the street. Lord Niddrie's clerk ran up to them, breathing heavily. 'What do you mean, sir, gieing me the slip like that?' He recognized Christine. 'Miss Murray, I hope you've not been frightened.'

'I nearly died of fear,' said Christine faintly, 'but I wouldna hae him ken it.'

'He's leagues away from both of us,' said the clerk. He took his master's arm, and tried to coax him away. 'Come away, sir. A bowl of brandy-punch at our own fireside – what do you say to that?'

The old man looked round vacantly, and shook the snowflakes from his wig. He let himself be guided up the street, and Christine heard the clerk talk to him as if to a fractious child, until they were out of earshot.

The encounter left her trembling; the old man's words fitted so exactly with her fears that they seemed like an omen of disaster. She forced herself to walk on, and reached the Netherbow Port without anyone else speaking to her.

The Port was the fortified gateway that marked the boundary between Edinburgh and the Canongate. Its towers rose out of sight into a thick swirl of snow, and the flakes hissed as they danced round the flaring torches on brackets at each end of its arched passage. Christine walked through, and waited for her father to come up Leith Wynd. Her feet and fingers ached with cold. She stared longingly at the chinks of light coming through the shutters of a nearby inn. She could almost feel the steamy, comforting warmth where she stood. She tried to imagine what Jamie would say if she told him she had gone into an ale-house to warm herself, and giggled hysterically.

She dared not approach the men coming up Leith Wynd. She watched their faces as they came near the arch, and she almost missed her father, who was walking between two other men. Luckily they stopped to say good-night to each other on the Canongate side of the Port.

'Christine!' exclaimed John Murray as she ran up to him. 'My daughter,' he explained to the two men, who stared at her, and pulled her away.

He seemed more amazed than shocked by her behaviour. Christine's story tumbled out incoherently, as she tried to explain what had happened about Ewan, and how frightened she was. She clung to her father's arm as they walked home.

'My dear lassie,' he comforted her, 'there was no need to come rushing out like this. He isna my brother. I could have borne to wait for this news.'

'Father, you dinna understand. Mr McDonnell is working for the Jacobites. He wants you to help him. He's dangerous, father!'

John Murray took her fears lightly. 'He canna force me to help him, my dear. I'll send him about his ways if he tries yon ploy.'

'He's so open about it,' she insisted. 'I'm sure the magistrates would soon arrest him. Would it not be wise to avoid him altogether?'

'Havers, Christine,' he scoffed. 'He may be in town for a few days only. I'd be blyth to hae a crack with him. Ewan's a wandering chiel. He came to join the Prince from France in forty-five, and there isna a court in Europe where he's not tried his fortune.'

He sounded so confident that Christine began to wonder if she had been too easily alarmed. She said no more about Ewan, but told him about her meeting with Lord Niddrie. It was hard to explain the horror this had caused her. John Murray was only amused.

'That'll teach you to go stravaiging in the dark!' he said.

After supper, Christine sat with her embroidery, and John Murray bent over Balmuir's map. He worked very slowly, and often stopped to stretch his fingers. He held the quill very stiffly; with anguish, Christine realized that it hurt him to use a pen. She had never realized before that the injury to his wrists might have affected the use of his hands. He must have spent many hours writing, during these past five weeks; yet he had never complained. She bit her lips, and turned away, unable to watch his painful effort. She was almost glad when Ewan tirled at the door, and he had to stop.

Ewan wore a gold-laced scarlet waistcoat, and carried an amber-headed cane. He entered with his arms held out, and the two men clapped each other on the shoulders, and cried out their delight at the meeting. Christine was relieved that Ewan hardly looked at her.

'You needn't give me your news,' said Ewan. 'I have it

all from the caddies. Forgive me for not calling sooner, but I had business yesterday.'

His manner seemed quite different now: it was open and jovial. He dismissed the past six years in a few words. He had been in Germany and France, he said, and the last eighteen months he had spent with the exiled Jacobite court in Rome.

John Murray asked what had happened to him at Fort Augustus, after he was captured.

Ewan laughed. 'It was an ugly experience. I escaped, and made my way to the coast. Then I took ship to the Low Countries.'

'You were more fortunate than others,' said John Murray grimly. He did not talk about his betrayal, or the snuff-box. He merely said that he had been taken to Tilbury, and there, he too had escaped.

Ewan shrugged. 'Those are old matters. I think little about the past. We must work for the future, John.'

Murray shook his head. 'The play's played, Ewan, and the song's sung. Dinna deceive yourself.'

'It is not over yet, John,' said Ewan eagerly. He brought from his pocket a copper medallion, the size of a penny. It had Prince Charles's head on one side, and on the other a withered oak-tree with a sapling growing beside it. The date 1750 appeared below the two trees, and round the edge was the inscription REVIRESCIT.

'See, John. "It grows green again." This is the Prince's Oak Medal, struck for the London Jacobites. There are great ploys afoot, man, and you should be working for us.'

'Ach!' exclaimed Murray disgustedly, 'there were great ploys in fifteen, and nineteen, and forty-five. Not for me again. The cause is dead, Ewan. The Stuarts will never come back to the throne.'

Ewan smiled and whispered his next words. 'Prince Charles was in London last year, inspecting the defences of the Tower.'

Murray rose in alarm. 'Wheesht, man.' He looked at

Christine. 'If you're to talk treason, at least let's hae the lassie out of the room.'

'Let her stay,' said Ewan airily. 'I daresay she's a better Jacobite than her father.'

Christine bent her head over her sewing. If only her father would tell Ewan to go away! But Ewan had caught his interest now, with his amazing news.

'*Treason*, John?' echoed Ewan. 'You didn't call it by that hard name when I met you at Perth. Listen. Twenty thousand muskets are to be laid ready at Antwerp. We shall seize the Tower and St James's Palace, with the help of three thousand supporters in London. The date is fixed for the tenth of November, next year.'

'Then what way are you up in Scotland?' asked Murray disbelievingly.

Ewan said that the north would rise for the Prince when London had fallen. He had come to contact Jacobite sympathizers among the Highland chieftains. There would be a great meeting of them next September, when the cattle drovers came to Crieff for the Michaelmas Tryst. There they would arrange the final details: for who would suspect they had any illegal reason for coming to the annual fair?

'Dr Archibald Cameron will come over next September, and so will me own cousin Lochgarry. From Edinburgh, I intend to find out which of the chieftains will rise for the Prince.'

Murray's face was grave. 'You're meddling with fire, Ewan.'

Ewan shrugged. 'I do not think so. We are grown more subtle these days, and I am not fool enough to throw myself into dangerous company. I write to the men I wish to contact, I do not meet them, and we have agents in the north. One of them works for the Linen Company in Perth.'

'I see!' cried Murray. 'Is that why you hae come to me?'

Ewan smiled and spread his hands. 'I cannot stay in

Edinburgh indefinitely, and I have instructions to make a link between this city and the north.'

Murray shook his head vigorously. 'Na, na, Ewan. You've come to the wrong man. I canna be a spy, even for the Prince.'

'You are afraid?' smiled Ewan.

Murray flushed. 'You should ken I'm no coward, Ewan. I hae other business to hand.'

'Fine business, too! You are a clerk, aren't you?'

'Aye,' said Murray quietly. 'I'm not ashamed of it. In a wee while I hope to farm some land again, even if it's not my own. I dinna want to waste my time loitering in taverns and making appointments with caddies.'

Ewan smiled once more. 'You have a strange notion of my occupation.'

'Maybe. I'm not feared to say that I value my life. I hae this lassie to think of, forbye. You can please yourself.'

'How do you intend to obtain this land?'

Murray looked uneasy. 'I shall save, then take a lease.'

'What!' scoffed Ewan. 'On your clerk's wages?' He looked down at the table, where Lord Balmuir's map was covered by the names which John Murray had so painfully marked on it. He slapped his hand across the document. 'John,' he said softly, 'I can show you a way to earn more silver in a month than you would ever win in two years, at your present wages.'

John Murray looked away, and put his head in his hands.

Christine, sewing by the fire, jabbed her finger. A cold, heavy weight seemed to press on her stomach as she saw how Ewan was beginning to work on her father, stirring up all the old despair and restlessness. Ewan did not understand her father's weakness; but he knew it was there, and was making use of it. Christine's hands began to tremble.

For some time Ewan looked at Murray's bowed head, with the same smile twisting his lips. Then he stood up briskly, as if the matter were finished. 'Come, let's have an end of these serious topics. Let's go to a tavern.'

Murray roused himself. 'I never go out after supper.'

Ewan slapped him on the back. 'Are you afraid some beau will run off with your pretty daughter? I am sure Miss Christine will excuse us. Besides, my throat is parched. If you have no wine in the house, I'll have to take you with me, or leave your company. Where is the best place to drink claret from the butt nowadays? Come, John, it isn't every day you meet an old comrade after six years' absence.'

He said this so winningly that John Murray could not refuse, and her father looked so pleased as he went out that Christine could not grudge him his amusement. She shuddered inwardly as Ewan gallantly claimed the Scottish privilege of kissing her cheek; but she submitted, for she was sure he would do it again to torment her if she showed her distaste. She wished them both a happy evening, and went to bed distraught with anxiety.

She realized that if her father had not enough strength of his own to resist Ewan, there was nothing she could do to help him. It all depended on how badly Ewan needed her father to help in his scheme. As she unpinned her gown, she wondered how persistent Ewan would be. She did not concern herself with the success or failure of the conspiracy. Foreign courts and their plots were too far away to touch her. She minded only what might happen to her father.

John Murray was out for a long time. The ten o'clock drum of the Town Guard had long since beaten through the town, and all the garbage had been thrown into the street, before he returned. Christine heard hands fumble at the door, then footsteps sounded inside the parlour. Through the curtain separating it from her bedroom, she saw a flash of light as a candle was lighted at the embers of the fire.

'How much money?' said her father's voice, thick and slightly slurred with wine.

'Twenty guineas – to begin with. Where did you say I left my cane?'

'By Christine's embroidery . . . When will I hae it?'

'Soon. I cannot say exactly. Your instructions will come next week. Good-night, John.'

'Good-night, Ewan.' The door opened and closed, and the light moved away. Christine heard her father go through to his own room, muttering to himself.

CHAPTER EIGHT

Letters

CHRISTINE found it hard to speak to her father at breakfast the next morning. As he rose to put on his hat and great-coat, he stopped beside her chair and tilted her face towards him.

'You're peelie-faced the morn, Christine. What ails you?'

'Nothing.' She pulled her face away.

'Did I disturb you when I came in last night?'

She rose hurriedly and began to clear the table. 'I dinna think I was waking then,' she said untruthfully.

John Murray watched her walk to and fro with the dishes. Then he said commandingly: 'Christine, come with me.' She followed him into the parlour, and he shut the door so that Lilias should not overhear them.

'Are you sure you didna hear me?'

Christine blushed and looked down.

'Since you did hear, you ken what I'm to do. Is that what fashes you?'

'You're doing it for *money*,' said Christine miserably. 'I believe you dinna care whether they succeed or no.'

'Why else should I do it?' he replied crisply. 'The Jacobites owe me some wages. Forbye, Christine, it's for the both of us, so that we can leave this stinking town.'

Her eyes filled with tears. 'You needna do it for me. I'd not hae you put yourself in danger for a mountain of silver. And I'm content to bide here.'

'So I'm thinking,' he answered with emphasis. 'But *I* am not content. I mean to do better than this; either in Scotland, or America, when I save our passage-money.' He pulled her down on the window-seat. 'See here, Christine.

I'm not a daft fool. I ken not to stick my neck in the rope. If the risk's ower great, I'll say "No".'

The words sounded fine. But he had said the same when he walked up the street with her last night. After a few hours in Ewan's company, he had pledged himself to the Jacobites again. She gripped the edge of the seat. 'What are you going to do for them?'

'A wee ploy connected with the Company's post-bags,' he smiled. 'Maybe you'll sleep better if you dinna hear the ins and outs of it.'

Christine fought not to show her panic. She might not be able to stop her father joining Ewan's scheme, but anything was better than not knowing what he intended to do. 'How did Mr McDonnell ken you were with the Company?' she demanded.

'He didna. He had a letter of introduction from their London office to Mr McCulloch. He saw my name on the lists by chance.'

Christine frowned. 'Why should he want to meet a Manager of the Linen Company?'

'He says it was some ploy thought up by the Chevalier's secretary in Rome. The Jacobites want to use the Company's organization for their own purposes, if they can. One of their agents already works for the Company in Perth.'

'Mr McDonnell said he had come straight here from Rome.'

John Murray raised his eyebrows. 'A man may travel to Edinburgh direct from Rome, and still hae to pass through London.'

'Oh.' Christine was abashed.

Her father laughed and patted her shoulder. 'You are a mistrustful creature, my dear.'

After he left the house, Christine thought over what he had said. The remark about the post-bags could only mean that Ewan had bribed her father to slip some letters of his own into the Company's mail. These were sent to the

Company's agents in the various towns where the Company had a correspondent.

Her father could only put Ewan's letters in the packet on a day when he was working in the Company's offices, and in charge of the mail. That would not be today: he had said he expected to spend the whole time at Little Picardy.

Christine's heart contracted as she realized what she must do. If Ewan had already handed over the letters they must be in her father's room. He would never risk carrying them round in his pocket until he put them in the postbag.

Her lips felt dry as she lifted the latch on the door of his room. Then she stepped back, and went through the passage to the kitchen.

'Lilias,' she said, 'can I trouble you to go to the markets today?' She rapidly discovered a plausible excuse. 'I want to write to Lady Strathdallin. I'll be at my father's desk if you want me.'

She waited until she heard Lilias close the front door, then went back to her father's room, which faced over Lady Drymen's courtyard. There was hardly any furniture there except the bed, a stool, and a worn armchair. The one pleasant object was a walnut writing-bureau. Like the silver candlesticks, it seemed to belong to a much more sumptuous household. The desk had been already supplied with quills, writing paper, ink and sand, when they arrived. As they did not care to move such a costly piece of furniture, her father allowed her to come in here when she wanted to write to Lady Strathdallin.

She lifted down the flap of the desk and set out the paper and seals. She wrote two sentences of her letter before she began her search.

There were hardly any places where the letters could be hidden. She looked into the clothes cupboard, in her father's chest, and even under the mattress. The letters were not there.

Reluctantly, she came back to the desk. Its drawers were not locked; this made her feel even more guilty. She could see nothing there except Lord Balmuir's map. When she pulled it out to look behind it, the copper medal that Ewan had shown her father rolled over the desk.

She was relieved that the letters were not there, but it was so important to find them that she searched again. She inspected the rows of drawers and pigeon-holes in front of her to see if she had missed anything.

One of the drawers seemed to have lost its small brass knob. But there was something strange about it: there was no mark where the knob should have been. She ran her fingers over the smooth walnut; the drawer-front was flush with the casing, and it was impossible to open it. She groped inside the nearest pigeon-hole, and found a small wooden button. When she pressed it, the drawer-front fell open. Inside was a bundle of letters.

Christine listened fearfully; but Lilias had not yet returned. As she grabbed the letters she wondered why one corner of the bundle was so badly burnt. Then she undid the old yellow tape that bound them, and eagerly smoothed out the first unsealed sheet. The words in the middle of the page were meaningless.

'I would have you bring the Hollands when next you ride to Perth, for your shirts are not so fine as I would have them. My father now admits that you are a handsome fellow. What do you say to that, sir?'

The letter was signed: 'Yr loving friend, Mary Drummond.'

Sick with disappointment, Christine thrust it away. She had found her mother's letters to her father. Lady Strathdallin must have sent them down by the same carrier who brought the necklace and rings for her birthday.

Then curiosity made her pick the letter up again. She knew it was wrong, but she already felt so guilty at searching the desk, that this was a small thing.

The letters dated from twenty years ago. Christine

realized with a shock that they began when her mother was exactly the same age as herself – sixteen. They were casual and teasing at first; for they were written to someone who was several years older than the writer. Then they changed into love-letters; there was one, written on the eve of the wedding when her mother was twenty, that had been added to in her father's writing. The words had been written after her mother's death. They repeated what Mrs Murray had said to her husband about Christine, shortly before she died.

Christine pushed the letter away, and began to weep quietly. The woman who wrote the letters was a stranger: she was weeping for this, more than because her mother had died.

And could her father really have been like this once, a young man who loved dancing and music, and was so gay that he finally won over dour old Mr Drummond, who had planned that his daughter should marry a rich Perth merchant? Perhaps the man she had expected to see in the Canongate stable-yard had existed once, after all.

He had been only a few years older than Jamie when these letters began. He had had no idea of the terrible things that would happen: that his wife would die when they had been married only seven years, that his home would be burnt, and that he would be driven into exile.

'I wish that the Prince had never come to Scotland,' whispered Christine fiercely to herself. She knew that she would do anything in the world to stop her father becoming involved again with the Jacobites.

There was a tap at the door. Christine hastily brushed her sleeve over her eyes, and bent over the letter she was supposed to be writing to Lady Strathdallin.

'Och, Miss Christine,' lamented Lilias, 'the food is getting terribly dear. The greens are scarce, and there is no meat to be had today forbye an old hen or two. It's coming on to snow again.'

Christine followed her to the kitchen and they unpacked the basket together. Lilias was unusually talkative.

'Now what do you think,' she cried, after the other gossip had been repeated. 'I saw that Mr McDonnell in the street, and he stopped to speak to me.' Her eyes were bright.

Christine looked at her sharply. 'Did he ask after my father?'

'Aye.' Lilias sounded disappointed, as if she had hoped that Ewan would talk of other matters. 'He says he has a packet of papers for the master, but he would not hand them over, no way at all.'

Christine began to slice angrily at the kail and other vegetables for the broth. 'Did he say when he'd come with them?'

'He just said he would cry in one of these days, and leave them if your father was not in.'

For several days after this, Christine found a good excuse for staying at home while Lilias did the shopping. The self-imposed restriction made her restless and irritable, but she dared not be away when the letters were delivered. She must either take them from Ewan herself, or see where her father put them when Ewan handed them over.

One day when it was too sleety to put the washing out on its pole, and she had a great heap of it steaming in front of the kitchen fire, there was a brisk rasping at the door. Christine's heart hammered violently.

But it was not Ewan. It was Henrietta.

She was muffled in a cloak with a fur-lined hood, and carried an enormous fur muff. 'Christine, let me in! I'm perished with the cold!' She darted past Christine.

'You'll hae to come to the kitchen,' apologized Christine. 'We dinna light the front room fire until the afternoon.'

Henrietta crouched down by the steaming clothes, rubbing her hands.

'I thought you were at Mrs Erskine's school the now,' said Christine.

'Aye, but whiles I just miss her classes.' She looked up at

Christine mischievously. 'Elizabeth is ower holy to miss a lesson. I thought I'd cry in for a wee crack. It's ages since we saw each other.'

'It's exactly a week,' Christine corrected her severely, touched, nevertheless, that Henrietta had come to see her. 'You were here after we went to the theatre.'

Henrietta pouted. 'Och, well, I was never a great hand at the mathematics. When are you coming to see us in the Canongate? My mother has a card-party next Tuesday; she doesna want Elizabeth and me with her company – so you come to us, and bring the French doll to show Elizabeth.'

They were still discussing the time of this visit when Henrietta gave a cry and jumped to the window. 'Look yon – wee Robin Lindsay, and the pig from under the stair!'

Down in the courtyard Robin was tottering after Jeanie and trying to catch hold of her tail. Jeanie was too interested in some old cabbage-stalks to move too far from him.

'Mrs Lindsay never lets him play in the courtyard,' said Henrietta. 'He'll take his death of cold.'

'Let's bring him in,' said Christine.

The two girls ran down the stair, along the narrow wynd, and so into Lady Drymen's courtyard. Jeanie took fright as they ran towards her, and trotted out of sight up Lady Drymen's stair. Christine picked Robin up.

'He's blue with cold,' she said. 'However did he get out?'

'By the back stair,' said Henrietta. 'I saw Sophia go into the library with Mrs Lindsay as I came along the street. The servant-lassie must hae let him out. Come this way.'

At the rear of the building, another turnpike stair went up as far as the Lindsay's flat. They rapped on the kitchen door; there was no answer. The kitchen was empty, but a pot was boiling on the fire.

'What'll we do?' asked Christine. In her arms, young Robin began to go to sleep. They heard a drone of voices from another room.

'That'll be Mr Lindsay,' said Henrietta, 'dictating a paper to his clerk. Should we disturb him?'

They looked at each other hesitantly. Then a tremendous shouting and squealing broke out in the courtyard below. First Jeanie hurtled through Lady Drymen's doorway, then the negro servant appeared, shouting and stamping his foot at the pig. She rushed towards the wynd, and a moment later they heard more noise and shouts towards the front of the house.

'I think we can go to Mr Lindsay now,' giggled Henrietta. 'I daresay he's been interrupted.'

They carried Robin to the front parlour. Mr Lindsay was peering out of the window and his clerk sat at a table, his quill poised in the air. The Lindsays' maid-servant burst into the room from the outside stair.

'What in Heaven's name is going on?' demanded Mr Lindsay, turning round to face her. The maid leapt to take Robin from Christine's arms, and they all began to talk at once. At last Henrietta talked everyone into silence, and explained what had happened.

'Dinna be fashed, sir,' gabbled the servant. 'I hadna enough greens for the pot, and I didna ken I'd left the door unsteekit behind me.' She rubbed the child's hands in great agitation.

'For goodness sake, Maggie, take him back to the kitchen with you. We hae to finish this paper by dinner-time ... Now what on earth is that?' he demanded in exasperated tones.

The noise had broken out afresh on the stair; at least half a dozen voices were calling up and down to each other.

'I think it's the pig,' said Maggie. 'Lucky said she'd gone, but I was that flustered about the bairn, I didna stop to hear.'

The stair door opened once again and in came old Mrs Lindsay, young Mrs Lindsay, and Sophia.

'You'll never guess what's happened!' cried Sophia excitedly. 'Jeanie's run mad. She's skelping up and down the stair, and they canna catch her.'

'Dinna tell such lees,' her grandmother rebuked her. 'The poor beast's dead scared with all those folk chasing after her. What a steer! I thought there must be a fire, when we came in.'

Mr Lindsay sighed, then made a sign to his clerk, who picked up the papers and slipped out, saying that he would meet him in the more peaceful surroundings of a tavern, and finish the paper in the afternoon. Mr Lindsay folded his arms resignedly, and prepared to waste the rest of the morning.

There were more explanations between Henrietta and young Mrs Lindsay, then Robin had to be fetched and fussed over to make sure he had not caught cold. The maid-servant could be heard crying in the kitchen, although no one had reprimanded her.

Still the noise outside continued. Then there was a rasping at the door, and Lucky Robertson put her head through.

'Excuse me, sirs, for being so unceremonious, but hae you seen our pig?'

'Hae you cried in on Lord Niddrie?' asked Mr Lindsay solemnly. 'He's very chief with Jeanie.'

They heard Lucky go up the stair, and the voices became quieter.

Mrs Lindsay the elder took off her cloak. 'My, Andrew, you're lucky that you can sit inby douce and quiet on a day like this. The cold would freeze your neb off. You'll not hae your golf-match if the weather doesna clear. This wind will blow you all into the Firth.'

'It's more likely to snow by then,' said young Mrs Lindsay.

'If there's snow on the Links,' said her husband, 'we'll play on the sands, like President Forbes used to do.'

There was another tirl at the door. It was Lucky again, with Jeanie tucked under her arm. 'You were right enough, sir,' she said. 'She was under his bed.' She looked round the crowded room, and said: 'Could I ask you a favour, sir?'

'Surely, Lucky. Ask on.'

'I hear the Greenshanks are a man short for their match on Saturday. I wonder – could I be so bold – would you hae *me*, sir?'

Mr Lindsay roared with laughter.

'I'm a braw hand with the clubs, sir,' Lucky persisted. 'Hae you ever seen me on Leith Links with the oyster-wives? I'm not so young as when I cried the fish up from Newhaven, but I can hit a ball as far as any man.'

Mr Lindsay eyed her brawny arms. 'Dod, I'll be sure of that ... Well, I'll ask our captain for you, Lucky. I'd be blyth to hae you with us.'

After she had gone, they all laughed. 'Oh, I'd like fine to see the match, Mr Lindsay,' cried Christine.

Henrietta clapped her hands. 'Why not? Let's take my father's chaise down to the Links. We'll take some food with us, and watch you play off.' Her face fell. 'Oh, I forgot. My mother said ... Mrs Lindsay,' she appealed to Jamie's mother, 'would you come with us, too? Christine and me, and Jamie and Geordie.'

Young Mrs Lindsay shook her head and smiled. 'What a daft idea, Hetty! Whoever heard of a pic-nic in December? Ask me again in the summer.'

Christine shared her cousin's disappointment. A daft idea, indeed, but it would have been delightful.

'We'll wrap up in furs,' coaxed Henrietta, 'and we'll run along the sands to keep warm.'

Young Mrs Lindsay shook her head again. 'Your father would never let the poor horses stand there while you had your pic-nic. The poor beasts would perish.'

'They could go to a stable in Leith. *Please*, Mrs Lindsay.'

Young Mrs Lindsay touched her cheek. '*No*, Hetty.'

Old Mrs Lindsay rapped the floor with her stick. There

was a glint in her eye. 'I'll go with the bairns to Leith,' she declared.

'Mother!' protested Mr Lindsay.

She turned on him warningly. 'Not a word, Andrew. I'll not hae you spoiling the bairns' pleasure.'

So Henrietta had her way.

That evening Ewan came back to see John Murray. He carried a small packet sewn up in red leather. Christine watched him put it on the table as if the packet would vanish the moment she took her eyes off it.

'You're ower late,' said Murray tersely. 'You wouldna tell me where you were off to, would you? I had to take the mail to the post-office on Tuesday.'

Ewan cursed. Then he controlled himself, and tapped the packet with the amber head of his cane. 'I suppose some more letters will go out soon?'

Murray grinned at his disappointment. 'Aye, but the snow will soon block the roads. I dinna ken if there will be more mail sent before the New Year now. Once the winter sets in the Company sends the mail by its own messengers. That's not so frequent as the public post.'

Ewan looked at him suspiciously. 'You must tell me about these new arrangements.'

'Aye – but I would like to see your silver first,' said Murray.

Ewan laughed contemptuously. 'Oh, is that all? Then tell me at least when you will know what the new arrangements are to be.'

'Maybe next week.'

'H'm,' said Ewan frowning. 'I have to go to Lord Elibank next week, so let us say I shall meet you next Saturday afternoon. I'll send you word about our meeting-place later. Meanwhile I'll take these back with me.' He put the red bundle into his pocket again.

'Make sure you bring the money too,' Murray reminded him.

'Never fear,' laughed Ewan. He picked up his hat and left.

John Murray put his arm round Christine's shoulders. 'There,' he said triumphantly, 'did I not manage him fine?'

Christine felt sick at heart. What did a few guineas more or less matter now? Ewan had won from the moment he persuaded her father to take part in his scheme.

'I think he means to trick you,' she replied.

'Let him try,' said her father ominously. 'If he doesna pay me, I ken where I'll send his letters. And it'll not be to the Jacobite agent in Perth.'

CHAPTER NINE

Leith Sands

AFTER Ewan had taken away the letters, Christine decided to think no more about them until she learnt where he would meet her father. She had not been out in the street for several days; now, on Thursday morning, she picked up the shopping basket eagerly. Lilias quickly pulled it from her hands.

'You dinna want to go outby on a cold day like this. I'll do the messages.'

Christine looked at her in astonishment. 'But you hate bargaining with market-wives, Lilias.'

Lilias' cheeks went pink. 'I am not caring now. Gie me the basket, Miss Christine.'

She was so insistent that Christine let her have it. The small incident nagged after Lilias had gone out. Lilias had taken a very long time to buy the few purchases she had been sent for during the last three days or so, although Christine had told her exactly where she would find the cheapest stalls. She remembered that one morning Lilias had come back with a message from Ewan. What if Lilias had gone out to meet him?

Christine anxiously put her 'tartan screen round her shoulders and ran down the stair. Lilias was out of sight; but almost certainly she had gone first to the kail-wives that sold vegetables round the Tron Church. Christine hurried down the hill, glancing left and right. There was no sign of Lilias in the street, or by the vegetable-stalls.

As she stood there in perplexity, she was greeted by Lucky Robertson's sister, who was sorting out an immense mound of frost-bitten kail.

'Is it your lassie you're after, my bairn? Go down to the

sedan-chairs. You'll find her with the Highland chairmen.'

Christine walked slowly past the wall of the church, where a row of sedan-chairs was neatly arranged by the north door. There, sure enough, was Lilias chattering in Gaelic to one of the chairmen, who seemed as delighted with Lilias's company as she was with his. He was a burly, handsome fellow; they were taking turns to sup a bowl of hot broth that had evidently come from the soup-stall a little way up the street.

Christine smiled to herself and went home. She decided not to mention what she had seen, but Lilias brought up the subject herself when she came back to Davidson's Land.

'I am after hearing a strange thing this morning. Whiles I stop to hae a word with the chairmen at the Tron Kirk. It is because of the Gaelic,' she added quickly. Christine stifled a smile. Lilias went on: 'One of them – his name is Donald McLaren, and a saucy fellow he is too,' she said with a smile that did not at all match her words, 'he is a brother to Kate, the widow of one of your father's crofters.'

There were more reminiscences, until Lilias reached her main piece of news.

'He is after hearing from his sister that some men have been busy round Strathdallin House with their notebooks and wee measuring lines. They have been round Tulmore, too. They were sent down by a mason in Perth. Would they be going to build the houses again, do you think?'

'I think your friend's sister is mistaken, Lilias,' said Christine. 'Lady Strathdallin said nothing about it in her last letter. Besides,' she added sadly, 'where would Lady Strathdallin find the silver to build Strathdallin House again?'

Lilias looked downcast. 'Maybe you are right. But Kate also wrote – or the minister wrote it for her, I should say, that a great sledgeful of logs was dragged to Strathdallin, and they are burning wood again in the big house, not only peat.'

'It's all blethers,' said Christine impatiently. Nevertheless she mentioned Lilias' news to her father.

He laughed. 'They'll be from the Linen Company. They mean to build a heckling mill by the river. All the same, it's strange they should be up there already. When I gied the map to Balmuir last night, he spoke as if they wouldna be up there until the spring.'

This conversation took place over supper on Thursday evening, after Christine had been to Mrs Lindsay's fortnightly tea-party. Her father had been home too late to join her, and he wanted to know who had been there, and what they had said.

'The old lady runs a fine clash-market,' he observed. 'She'll not miss a piece of gossip in the whole town.' He looked at Christine expectantly.

'I suppose not,' she replied warily. 'I hardly spoke to her myself.' It was true. She had spent most of her time discussing the picnic at Leith with Henrietta and Jamie. The plan was becoming more and more elaborate. Henrietta now intended to ask her father to lend them the coach-and-six instead of the chaise, and they were going to have a bonfire on the sands.

John Murray began to eat the fruit tart that Lilias had baked for supper. 'This is gey tasty,' he said with appreciation, then suddenly: 'Does she ken Mrs Patterson?'

Christine was bewildered. 'Who, father?'

'Mrs Patterson, the wife of the goldsmith in Parliament Close. Did Mrs Lindsay speak of her?'

'No,' she said in astonishment.

'I think I'll hae a word with Mrs Lindsay about her.'

Christine went pale. 'Father, she'd ken you were after something. It would look so strange. Please dinna ask her.'

'What does it matter to you?' he demanded coolly.

Christine looked at him wretchedly. 'I dinna want the Lindsays brought into it.'

He helped himself to more tart. 'Then ask her yourself. You ken her well, you could draw the old lady on, and she'd never notice.'

'I'll do nothing of the kind!' she cried passionately.

'You'll hae a fine opportunity when she takes you all to Leith. Now, Christine, either you find out who Mrs Patterson was with in the winter of forty-five, or I'll ask her myself, next week.'

'It's not fair!' she said miserably.

'It's no use, my dear. I mean to find out, whatever the Lindsays think of us.' There was a hardness about him that she had never seen before. 'Which is it to be?' he demanded.

'I'll ask her,' she muttered, hating him because he had forced her to give the promise, and wanted to spoil the afternoon she had so much looked forward to.

On the day of the match, the Greenshanks assembled outside Davidson's Land with their golf-clubs and leather balls. Each of them wore green stockings and a curly pig's tail pinned like a cockade to his hat. The passers-by grinned, but they were used to the fanciful dress of the Edinburgh clubs.

Christine saw Lucky come out of her pie-shop wearing a fishwife's striped petticoat. The men raised a huzza and waved their hats. Then they all marched off towards the Links, and Lucky stepped proudly at their head.

The Greenshanks were going to meet their rivals at Straiton's tavern in Leith before the match, which would begin at half-past two. A caddy had been sent down early to Leith, and reported that snow was lying on the Links; so the match had to be shortened, and they would play as well as they could across the sands.

At noon Christine walked with old Mrs Lindsay to the Canongate stables, where they had arranged to meet Jamie, Henrietta, and Geordie. Jamie met them, emerging from College Wynd, and they walked to the North Back of the Canongate, to Laurence Ord's Close. Under the huge vaulted entrance to the stables stood the Balmuir family coach. It was much bigger than the chaise. Henrietta leaned out excitedly as they appeared.

'Hurry!' she cried.

The stable-boys led out the six horses, and harnessed them, then stood back grinning as the coachman appeared, heading a procession of servants with large hampers and a pile of fur wraps.

'Mercy on us, Henrietta,' cried Mrs Lindsay, 'what's in those baskets? I hope you dinna mean us to encamp for the night.'

'It's only a slight collation,' said Henrietta importantly. '*Do* climb in. I'm fidgeting to start.'

Jamie handed in his grandmother and Christine, and Henrietta swathed them both in furs. Jamie bent over the Balmuir crest and arms gilded on the door. 'I yield neither to heat nor cold,' he quoted, translating the Latin phrase as he stepped in. 'Hetty, I dinna think there'll be much heat to frighten you today.' He blew on his hands and thrust them deep in his pockets.

'You've forgotten the bonfire,' said Henrietta triumphantly. She whispered to Mrs Lindsay. 'Did you do it?'

'Oh, yon.' Mrs Lindsay chuckled. 'Aye, I did.'

'What's that?' asked Christine, violently curious.

'You'll just hae to bide and see,' laughed the old lady, and exchanged a smile with Henrietta.

The coachman cracked his whip, and the heavy vehicle lumbered into the street. There was a shout and thudding footsteps, and Geordie, scarlet-faced, scrambled into the coach.

'You meant to go without me!' he accused his sister.

'Na, na,' replied Henrietta. 'You promised to be here to direct the servants carry the food. Where hae you been?'

Geordie pulled the fur rug up to his ears. With his plump cheeks and fair curling hair, he looked rather like a chicken, Christine thought, fluffing its feathers against the cold. 'It's Ajax. He's off his meat. I was trying to coax him into eating.'

Henrietta shuddered. 'Would *you* eat, if you were to be killed next Saturday afternoon?'

'He stands a fair chance,' said Geordie hotly.

'Yon big Murchiston bairn has one that will swinge him,' said Jamie. 'Your Ajax is feared to use his spurs.'

Christine realized that they were talking about a fighting-cock. The two boys discussed Ajax's chances for several minutes. Henrietta, casting up her eyes, explained that there was a match between the students and the High School boys next week, behind a Cowgate tavern, and fourteen cocks would be fighting.

Mrs Lindsay took some snuff as she listened to the two boys. 'I mind the match last year,' she said. 'It ended in a bicker between the collegers and the school-bairns, and there was more blood from broken noses than from the cocks themselves. It's a pity you dinna fight with geese, Geordie. Then we'd hae the poor dead fugies to put into a goose-pie for our Yule. When I was a lassie the country-folk around Ayr aye had their goose-pie at Yule. The minister used to come round to see what they had put by for their "Christmas". A terrible heathen feast, he called it. He'd put the old wives on the stool of penitence the next Sabbath if he found anything.'

She rambled on; Christine forgot what she had promised her father, and half-listened to Mrs Lindsay's stories, and half-watched the outline of Jamie's head against the snowy landscape outside. The coachman took the horses at a cautious walk down the hill; the buildings fell away, and the brown and grey of frozen slush gave way to sparkling white; white on Arthur's Seat behind them, white tipping the hills of Fife across the water, and white flecks on the waves that ran up Leith sands.

They passed the Links where one or two glum-looking golfers were walking round with their clubs over their shoulders. Sometimes the golfers would drag their toes through the snow, as if to make sure the turf was still there beneath it.

'I kent it would be fine!' cried Henrietta. 'Look at yon blue sky, and there's hardly a sooch of wind.'

They found two Balmuir footmen building a fire of driftwood on the sand at the roadside. The men waved when the coach appeared; they said reproachfully to Henrietta that some folk had been over to them already and asked if they were setting up a signal for smugglers.

Henrietta laughed at them, and told them to go home. The two boys lifted out the hampers, while the coachman and postilion unharnessed the horses and took them to a stable in Leith until the end of the afternoon.

The seagulls wheeled overhead with shrill cries as Henrietta unpacked the picnic: a game-pie and a syllabub, legs of chicken, slices of turnip for a relish; wine for Mrs Lindsay, ale for the boys, cordial for Christine and herself.

Mrs Lindsay sat in the coach, but the young people ate outside, jumping up and down to keep warm. Henrietta pulled a saucepan and a wine-bottle filled with milk from under the seat. She took some ale and wine and added it to the milk to make a posset, then stood the saucepan at the edge of the fire. It wobbled a little; but soon the liquid was sizzling in the copper pan. Although there were specks of ash in it, they were thankful for its scalding warmth.

'That was my own idea,' said Henrietta, as she handed some to Mrs Lindsay. 'Mama doesna ken I hae the pan out of the kitchen.'

'Here they come to begin the match,' said Geordie.

Two figures with golf-clubs strolled across the empty stretch of sand. Behind them walked the caddy who had followed John Murray down the High Street. One of the golfers threw a small leather ball on to the sand, and practised a shot.

'They're not wearing green stockings,' said Jamie. 'They must be two from the other club, the Sons of Wallace.'

Mrs Lindsay peered out of the window. 'I dinna think

so. Christine, is that not the man I saw on the stair on Wednesday night, going up to your door?'

It was Ewan. Christine moved back out of sight, her pleasure spoilt by seeing the hateful figure.

'He came to see my father,' she admitted reluctantly. 'He fought beside my father at Culloden.'

Mrs Lindsay stared at the two men. 'He keeps fine company. Yon's the Lord Justice-Clerk with him. He canna be much of a Jacobite now, when he foregathers with a High Court officer.'

Christine's heart beat fast with fear, in case Mrs Lindsay began to question her about Ewan. The two men were deep in conversation; their game of golf seemed much less important to them than whatever they were talking about.

They soon disappeared across the sand; but one fear was replaced by another, as she remembered that she had to ask Mrs Lindsay about the goldsmith's wife. She waited anxiously for her opportunity.

The Greenshanks appeared at last. The two boys started to walk towards them, and Henrietta followed. Christine stepped into the carriage with Mrs Lindsay.

'Bide there, Hetty,' said Jamie. 'We'll find out where they're to set the course, then we'll come back to tell you.'

To Christine's annoyance, Henrietta climbed among the furs with her.

The crowd of golfers was not very large. Later Christine heard that the fireside of Straiton's tavern had been too much of a temptation for some, and they had refused to come out for the match. Two or three more, led by Dr Herries, had gone off to sample the prawns and chestnuts served with wine at the Old Ship inn. Several of the Sons of Wallace had weakly succumbed, too, so the numbers were even, and only half a dozen pairs were there for the match.

'What are the laddies doing?' asked Henrietta, leaning out of the window. Jamie and Geordie were running along the sand, stooping now and then to do something at their feet whenever one of the Greenshanks waved his arms at them.

'They must be putting in the holes,' said Mrs Lindsay.

'They're sinking them in with oyster-shells!' exclaimed Christine. She watched Jamie run back to take a bundle of rods and some brightly-coloured rags from his father. He retraced his steps, planted a rod by each hole, and tied on a piece of rag.

Henrietta wriggled excitedly. 'There's Lucky Robertson. I must go and see what's happening. Christine, come with me!'

'I'll come in a moment, when they begin.'

'Off with you,' said Mrs Lindsay briskly. 'I'll just sit still and keek out of the window.' When they were left alone, she looked at Christine with a slightly malicious twinkle in her eye.

'Well, my bairn, what's this you're so anxious to ask me?'

Christine gasped in horror.

The old lady cackled, and prodded her in the ribs. 'It's written large in your face, lassie. You've been looking asklent at me for the past ten minutes. Either you've burnt a hole in my sheets with the candles, or you hae a question to put to me. Out with it.'

Christine gulped, not knowing where to look. There was no point in leading gradually to the subject now.

'Do you ken Mrs Patterson, the goldsmith's wife?'

'Aye, her husband is Lady Balmuir's jeweller. What about her?'

Christine's fingers twisted unhappily round the edge of the fur wrap. 'I'd like to ken – I'd like to ken if you knew her family in forty-five. You see –' She stammered and blushed, and her voice completely left her. Her hands were shaking.

Mrs Lindsay watched her calmly for several moments, then patted her arm. 'You'll notice that I dinna put any questions to *you*. I'd rather not hear why you're asking this, for I ken fine you're not putting the questions for yourself. Dinna look so downcast: you'd hae to be gey smart to outwit an old body like myself.' She opened her snuff-box, and took a large pinch. 'Anyways, you might as well save your breath. I hadna left Pitcairnie in forty-five.'

Christine forgot her confusion, filled with relief that Mrs Patterson's secret could not be given away by Mrs Lindsay. But she was puzzled.

'I thought you were at the Prince's ball in Holyrood, in forty-five.'

'Aye, was I. But Lady Drymen sent me word at Pitcairnie that she'd beg me an invitation if only I'd come to stay six-seven days with her in Edinburgh. What a trauchle I had to leave Pitcairnie!' She laughed to herself as she remembered.

'Why was that?' asked Christine.

'The laird – he's my eldest laddie, Robert – didna want me to come, nor his wife Helen, either. They wouldna let me hae a carriage, and they almost locked me in my room. But I jinked them,' she said gleefully. 'Jamie was a High School bairn then, and he was on his holidays at Pitcairnie. He locked the laird and his wife in their bedroom while they slept, then he went for the carter in the village. I rode pillion with the carter on one horse, and we put my ball-gown and nightshift on the other, and we rode all the way to the Kinghorn ferry. What a belting Jamie had from his uncle when he found that I had gone!'

Christine laughed. 'I canna see Jamie doing a thing like that.'

Mrs Lindsay gave her a sly look. 'He's a romantic chiel under all that gravity. If he'd do all that for a daft old body like me – what would he not do for *you*, Christine?'

Christine blushed, looked away, then felt pride and happiness swell inside her like water bubbling up the side of a glass. She kept on laughing, and the colour came and went in her cheeks until she was sure that Mrs Lindsay must think she was mad. But the old lady only laughed with her, squeezed her hands and said:

'So you see, my dear lassie, I canna tell you about Mrs Patterson.'

Her cousins and Jamie returned at that moment, and said that the golfers were beginning their match. Mrs Lindsay told her to join the others, and Christine jumped on to the sand, not daring to meet Jamie's eyes.

Lucky Robertson and the captain of the Sons of Wallace were about to drive off. Lucky drove twenty yards beyond her rival, a great feat on the soft sand. The other couples drove off behind them.

It was very cold standing there to watch the golfers, and an icy breeze began to flutter the rags on the markers.

'Let's hae a race,' said Henrietta. She ran down to the edge of the sea with amazing speed, and stood waving her muff derisively until the others joined her. She began to chant:

> 'To Noroway, to Noroway,
> To Noroway ower the faem;
> The King's daughter of Noroway,
> 'Tis thou maun bring her hame.'

'Where's Noroway?' asked Geordie.

Henrietta waved seawards. 'There, somewhere beyond the Bass Rock. Let's race again.'

'Let's fetch some dry seaweed for the fire,' said Jamie. 'There's a fine lot of it by those rocks.' He seized Christine's hand. 'We two will race you two.'

'Geordie canna run,' protested Henrietta, but she took her brother's hand all the same, and tugged him on in a vain effort to keep up with Jamie and Christine.

The salt stung Christine's cheeks as she ran along the edge of the water with Jamie. She twisted round to look at him, and the ribbon slipped from her hair. 'My hair!' she cried breathlessly. 'It's coming down.'

'Never mind,' he laughed, pulling her on. 'It suits you fine.'

She clutched at her hair with her free hand, but it tumbled round her shoulders, and when they stood panting by the rocks, waiting for Henrietta and Geordie, it whipped round her face in the wind and she had to hold it back with her fingers.

'You look like a wild witch,' Jamie teased her, and pulled back a strand that blew across her eyes. As his fingers brushed her cheek something leapt inside her, and her legs trembled.

'Jamie.'

'Yes, my dear?' He smiled at her.

'I wish this afternoon could go on and on.'

He laughed, but his eyes were affectionate as he looked at her.

'Is that what you really want, Christine?'

She was too shy to explain what she meant. Something warned her that it had to be kept secret; that Jamie was the last person she could tell, until he found it out for himself. Her happiness blazed inside her as she uttered the very ordinary words:

'I dare say not. We'd all perish of the cold.'

Henrietta came up with Geordie, holding out her hand. 'Here's your ribbon, Christine. It nearly blew into the sea.'

Christine tied back her hair, then they scooped up armfuls of the dry seaweed and returned to the bonfire. They tossed the armfuls on, and watched the flames spurt into a shower of blue sparks as they caught the dried salt. Then they went back to watch the golfers.

In another half-hour, the game was over, and the Greenshanks had won by three matches.

Most of the golfers went back to Leith, but Mr Lindsay and Lucky and two of the Sons of Wallace stayed by the bonfire, although the light was waning. The beach became quiet, and the sea-birds vanished.

Henrietta looked anxiously along the road. 'Why does he not come? My surprise will be too late.'

A single horseman appeared on the road, bouncing awkwardly in his saddle. Christine recognized the music-teacher she had seen at Balmuir House when she first met her cousins.

Signor Rosalbo slid off his horse and unstrapped his fiddle. He bowed to old Mrs Lindsay. 'Madam, I am here as you asked me.'

She drew the furs around her. 'Right, just one dance to please the bairns, for the mirk is coming on and it's bitter cold.'

Signor Rosalbo blew on his fingers and drew as near the bonfire as he could without scorching his coat. 'Something lively, no, to warm you? Let me play a reel I have composed myself. This will be its first performance. I call it "The Edinburgh Reel".'

He flourished his bow and tucked the fiddle under his chin; then he struck up the music. Mrs Lindsay nodded her head, and tapped her stick on the floor of the carriage. The four young people, Mr Lindsay, Lucky, and the two Sons of Wallace formed up opposite each other on the sand. Jamie took Christine for his partner.

Their feet and arms flashed against the bonfire, their cries rang across the empty beach as they whirled and stamped through the figures of the reel. Jamie linked arms with Christine in the centre of the circle.

'Do you ken this,' he called over his shoulder, '*I'd* like the afternoon to go on and on!'

CHAPTER TEN

The Cock-Fight

THE front room was dark when Christine entered the house, although the fire was already blazing on the hearth. She groped towards the shelf where the rushlight stood in its holder, then halted, stiff with horror. She could hear voices speaking Gaelic in the kitchen. The exaltation of the afternoon vanished. What could she say, if she found Ewan there? Disgustedly, she lit the rushlight, and went along the passage. She had to make sure that she received the letters.

Lilias jumped up, and so did the man with her. They had been toasting bannocks by the fire, and there was a mug of ale standing between them. But the man was not Ewan.

'Miss Christine,' whispered Lilias in a choked voice, 'I did not think you would be back this long while.'

The man turned his bonnet round in his hands. He seemed to fill the small kitchen. 'I had better be away,' he said. He was Donald MacLaren, the chairman.

Christine was more embarrassed by their embarrassment, than by the fact that she had broken in on such a private scene.

'Dinna go,' she said. 'I'll sit in the parlour until my father comes home.'

They all looked at each other; Christine wondered why the man who built Davidson's Land had not provided a back stair to the upper flats. Perhaps he did not think that servants should be allowed to entertain their friends in their masters' kitchens. If Donald stayed now, he would have to walk through the parlour when he left.

Donald went to the door. 'Thank you, Miss Murray, but

I think I shall go,' he said, with stately politeness. 'I have promised to take Lady Drymen to a card party at seven o'clock, and I must find my boy.'

When he had gone, Christine pretended to look for a linen cap among a heap of freshly-ironed clothes. She wanted to give Lilias time to recover from her embarrassment.

'Did Donald hae more news from his sister at Strathdallin?' she asked, for something to say.

Lilias became very busy about the knife-box. 'Aye; the carpenter has been to Strathdallin House, and he is to make six wooden boxes for the mistress. He said to Kate that Lady Strathdallin would be leaving home soon.'

'Is that so?' commented Christine, with a smile. She let Lilias give her a few more items of gossip, then went back to her embroidery in the parlour.

John Murray did not come home until nine o'clock. He had been kept late packing some samples of yarn and linen that the Company wanted to dispatch to their agents in the north.

'Mr McCulloch wants them to hae these by them when the spinning-schools open, to show the French methods. And we want the weavers to bleach their cloth in the new way – with a chemical from the new vitriol factory at Prestonpans.'

'Does that gie a better bleach than the butter-milk?' asked Christine.

'Far and away better. Mr Black, the chemist, told us to try it.'

Then he asked her how she had spent the afternoon. He smiled as she described the pic-nic and the golf-match. At last she came, reluctantly, to the matter of Mrs Patterson, and said that Mrs Lindsay could tell her nothing.

He seemed only a little disappointed. 'Och,' he shrugged, 'I dare say I'll find out some other way.' He began to talk again about the new process for bleaching linen, as if the whole matter of the snuff-box were now of little importance.

Christine did not mention that she had seen Ewan on the Links.

Two days later a message was brought for her father. She opened the door to see the caddy whom she had last seen walking behind Ewan on Leith sands. There was something eerie about the way he kept appearing, and she took the letter from him with distaste.

She knew at once the note would be from Ewan. It was unsealed, rashly open for anyone who might care to read it. Yet how evasive Ewan was when her father questioned him about his movements, or asked who had sent him to Edinburgh! There was a strange contradiction about his behaviour.

Christine took the precaution of seeing that Lilias was well-occupied, then unfolded the letter.

'Sir: I shall see you next Saturday as we arranged. I hear there is to be a main between the schoolchildren and the students at Strang's tavern. Cocking is a sport I dearly love, and have been deprived of for some time. So will you give me a wager?'

The letter was signed only with Ewan's initials, with the additional sentence: 'Three o'clock exactly.'

At least there was nothing incriminating in the letter, even if the caddy had read it. Christine refolded it, and put it on her father's desk.

Her father seemed to have reached a position of some importance in the Linen Company, and his working hours had become very irregular. So there was no doubt he would be able to keep this appointment with Ewan.

All day she tried to think of some plan. There was no point in stealing the letters when Ewan handed them over. She realized that now. Either Ewan would do something terrible to her father, or give him copies to send with the next post-bag. No: she must discover more about their plans before she decided what to do. She would have to follow her father to the cock-fight.

At first the idea seemed foolish. Then, as she thought about it, it became more acceptable. Even if her father or Ewan saw her at the fight she could easily find some excuse for being there. She could say that she had come to watch cousin Geordie. She could even say that she had come with Jamie.

Christine's cheeks flushed, and her eyes shone. She would go out to meet Jamie before he came home at noon on Saturday.

Just before St Giles struck twelve on Saturday morning, she went down the stair. Young Mrs Lindsay put her head out of her door as Christine passed by.

'My dear, you must hae read my thoughts. I hae some bonny new silks from the Lawnmarket to show you. Come away in and see if you'd like any for your embroidery. I was just about to step up to you myself.'

Biting her lip with vexation, Christine followed Mrs Lindsay into the flat. The silks were indeed pretty; she could not tear herself away without being rude, and her heart sank as she heard the door open.

Jamie's face lighted up when he saw Christine.

'Jamie, I'm blyth to see you,' said his mother. 'Your father's at the tavern with his writer, and Maggie is down at the meal market. I want to go to the circulating library. Mrs Innes tells me there's a grand new novel called *Harriot Stuart* and she's just cried in to say she returned it to Mr Ramsay this morning.'

'You and your romantic novels, mother!' laughed Jamie.

She reached up to tap him on the cheek. 'Wait till you've brought up four peenging bairns, James Lindsay, and you'll ken why I read them.' She put on her tippet and hat, and left them alone.

Here was her opportunity, and Christine seized it.

'Jamie, will you do me a favour?'

'Of course,' he said warmly.

'Will you take me to the cock-fight this afternoon?'

He looked startled, and what was worse, even a little disgusted, she thought. 'Well . . .' he said doubtfully.

She tried to make a joke of it. 'Is this something else a young lady must not do?'

He frowned, and said curtly: 'Why do you want to go?'

'Och, I just took a notion to it,' she said airily to hide her dismay. 'Do you not go yourself?'

'I used to, at school. Not now.'

'Why not now? Do you not want to see Geordie win?'

Jamie looked very embarrassed. 'Well, if I hae to tell you –' he began gruffly, then burst out: 'I dinna like it! It's a foul thing, and I'll not watch the birds suffer.'

Christine looked at him curiously. 'Are you feared of the blood?'

'No!' he shouted.

'I had to kill the hens at Strathdallin. I didna like it, but I did it as quick as possible. Anyways, folk say that the cocks enjoy fighting.'

'Aye – till they're wounded, poor beasts.' He looked at her very shamefacedly. 'Christine,' he begged, 'you'll not tell Geordie or your other cousins what I said just now? They'd laugh at me.'

'Of course I'll not.' She was surprised and touched to find this weakness in him. It was rather unmanly, she thought, but she liked him for it.

Jamie seemed relieved at her promise, then said: 'You'll not go there, will you, Christine?'

She had put herself into a false position, but there was no drawing back now. 'I think I will,' she said carelessly. 'I'd like fine to see a cock-fight.'

She was distressed to see how disgusted he looked. His tone became rough, as if she had disappointed him in some way. She was thankful when Mrs Lindsay returned from the library. When Christine left them, Jamie opened the door, but he did not look at her. She ran upstairs, nearly in tears.

She went down to the tavern just before three o'clock. The yard was filled with schoolboys and students. There were some older men there as well, writing down the bets in small notebooks, and a man who looked like the inn-keeper, who seemed to be supervising the wagers. He sat on a chair at the ringside, and held a box full of copper coins and bank promise-to-pay notes on his knees.

The main had not yet started. Seven schoolboys, seven students, all clustered at the edge of the cock-pit carrying their birds in wicker baskets. Geordie had taken out Ajax, and was adjusting his spurs. The bird screeched and kicked, and Geordie yelled as the steel blade gashed his hand.

Christine squeezed to the back of the crowd. There were no other women there except the serving-maids from the tavern; but the crowd was too excited to pay her much attention. She saw Captain Binning there; he elbowed his way to the landlord, and thrust some money into his box. Then he fell back, and Christine lost sight of him.

'Last wagers, gentlemen, last wagers on the first match!' shouted the landlord. One of the students and one school-boy stepped across the barrier and crouched at opposite sides of the pit with their cocks between their hands. The birds looked small: their combs and feathers had been clipped for fighting. But they jabbed their necks fiercely towards each other, and struggled to be free.

'Set them to!' shouted the landlord.

The two boys approached each other cautiously, and held the birls while they pecked at each other's beaks. Then they jumped back and climbed across the barrier. The cocks flapped their wings with hoarse cries, and began to slash each other with spurs and beaks. Their feathers were soon soaked with blood, but they went on fighting until one ran round blindly, unable to see, and the other had fallen over with a broken leg.

Christine shut her eyes and felt very sick.

'Set them to again,' ordered the landlord. The two boys

jumped in and set the cocks breast to breast. They pecked feebly, but the fight was over. 'Hae them out without a count,' said the landlord impatiently. 'We'll cry it a draw. Next pair in.'

Christine saw her father come into the yard and look around. He pushed his way to the front, and stood watching the second fight. Christine kept her eyes on the entrance, and in a few moments Ewan came in too. He caught sight of John Murray, waved his cane, and made his way towards the barrier. Christine forced her way forwards so that she could stand just behind them. She tried not to see what was going on in the pit. A fat man, in a leather apron, who smelt abominably, made way for her with a remark that Christine pretended not to hear. He laid his hands familiarly on her shoulders, but she was afraid to make a fuss in case she was noticed by Ewan or her father.

The yells of the crowd half-drowned what they said to each other, but she managed to hear the gist of it.

'I have the letters.' Ewan tapped his pocket. 'Also the money.' He brought out a handful of coins and notes, which John Murray took with his eyes still on the fighting-cocks.

'What's the new plan for the Company's mail?' asked Ewan.

'We're sending some samples up to Perth and the Company letters with them. They will all go next Thursday morning.'

'How?' demanded Ewan.

'Balmuir's chaise will – hey, you swicking deil! I thought it was to be twenty guineas.' He turned furiously towards Ewan, as far as the press of knees and elbows would let him.

'Strong words between gentlemen, John. Did I say twenty?'

'Aye, did you. Here's only ten.'

Ewan smiled. 'I remember now. I will bring the other ten later. Meanwhile, here are the letters.'

For the first time his gestures became furtive. He pressed against Murray's side, and without looking down tucked the small leather parcel into the other man's pocket. Murray looked straight ahead as he did this.

'Ewan, Balmuir's chaise is to take the samples and letters to Perth. I hae to put them in the chaise the night before it goes there. I swear your letters will not go with the rest unless you gie me the money by Wednesday night.'

'You'll have your money,' laughed Ewan scornfully. 'Now let us enjoy the main.'

'Why, there's my cousin George Grant!' exclaimed Murray.

Christine saw Geordie crouched on the far side of the cock-pit, a look of fierce determination on his face. He bent down and stroked Ajax's back feathers, whispering as if the bird could understand him.

'How can he bear to see him fight if he likes him so well?' Christine asked herself in amazement.

Geordie's opponent held a huge, vicious-tempered cock that looked twice the size of Ajax. The boys set them to, then jumped back. Ajax crowed and flapped, but he jerked back his neck timidly as the other bird swooped over him with a terrible scream of rage. In another moment the other bird was chasing him round the pit.

'A fugie, a fugie!' jeered the High School boys. 'Take him out.'

'He's not!' Geordie shouted back in wrath.

'Make him fight then, my lad,' called out Captain Binning. The two owners jumped into the pit and set the birds breast to breast. The large cock beat with his spurs and wings like a fury; in a moment Ajax was struggling on the ground, as his enemy kicked his spurs again and again into his breast. His blood dribbled on the ground, and splashed the sides of the barrier.

Christine shuddered with pity for the helpless bird being

gored to death. Why could they not declare the other bird the victor and take poor Ajax out? Everyone went on shouting; even Geordie only waved his arms and cried: 'Ajax, Ajax, stand up and fight!'

With shame Christine remembered how she had thought Jamie rather squeamish when he refused to come to the fight. She felt she would vomit at any moment, but she could not go to the yard entrance without passing in front of her father. She tried not to look; but there was a dreadful fascination in the convulsions of the dying bird.

Ewan and her father were bending over the barrier. Ewan suddenly jerked upright and stared across the cockpit at Captain Binning. 'I must leave you, John,' he said in an agitated voice.

'Before the main is finished?' asked Murray in disappointment. 'Forbye, there's more to tell you about the letters.'

Ewan hesitated. 'Oh, very well. Let's talk in the alehouse.'

He turned round so abruptly that Christine hardly had time to dodge out of sight behind the fat man. Ewan pushed to the back of the crowd and walked round three sides of the yard to reach the tavern door. John Murray followed him on this strange route.

Christine wondered why the sight of Captain Binning had alarmed Ewan. She tried to edge towards the yard entrance, but found it impossible. Geordie jumped into the cock-pit and picked up the limp, mangled body. The landlord held out his hand.

'All fugies go to the kitchen. You ken the rules, Mr Grant.'

Geordie glowered. 'I want to take him home.'

The High School boys jeered and shouted. 'You canna, he's a fugie.' They far outnumbered their rivals, for few of the students had turned up to support their seven cock-fighters.

The fat man nudged Christine. 'My bonny doo, I'd

make out of here as quick's you can. There's going to be a bicker, and if the Town Guard arrives, we'll all land in the gaol.'

The schoolboys and students began to jostle each other angrily; the older men left the yard quickly or retreated into the inn. The landlord grabbed his box of stake-money and ran after them, slamming the back door behind him.

The boys started to hit each other and kick the cock-baskets round the yard. The remaining birds screeched and flew on to the roof. In a moment there was a raging battle: the students were heavier than the schoolboys, but the odds were against them.

As Christine tried to rush out of the yard she saw three schoolboys set on Geordie, and one of them gave him a sounding crack on the nose. Geordie staggered against the wall; blood gushed through the fingers he clapped to his face.

Christine ran back across the yard and hammered on the backdoor of the inn. It was cautiously opened a few inches.

'My father's inby!' she cried desperately. 'Please let me in!'

The landlord pulled her through and slammed the door again. Christine's eyes smarted in the thick reek of coal-smoke and tobacco. The benches were crowded, and the room was dark because the one small window was blocked with the heads and shoulders of men watching the struggle in the yard.

Christine pushed her way over to her father and Ewan. 'Father, come quickly! There's cousin Geordie being murdered by three other laddies.'

John Murray gave her an astonished glance but did not stop to ask what she was doing there. 'Are you coming to help, Ewan? We'll dunt these youngsters' heads together.'

'Not I,' laughed Ewan, 'I don't want to meddle with the Town Guard.'

Christine followed her father back into the yard. John Murray strode into the middle of the fight. The three schoolboys were dancing round Geordie, and kicking him as they dodged the barrel stave he defended himself with. John Murray took the youngest boy by the waist and threw him across the yard; then he hooked his leg round the shin of the next, and pulled him to the ground.

'Now for you, my birkie!' he panted, turning to the third and largest. The boy ducked his head and started to charge; then he thought better of it and stood back, just as the Town Guard marched into the yard.

The fighters scattered like mice, but the guardsmen laid their Lochaber axes across the yard entrance, and herded the boys into the middle. John Murray seized Geordie's arm and dragged him up to the sergeant.

'I'll be responsible for this lad,' he announced. 'He is the son of my cousin, Lord Balmuir, and I wish to take him home.'

The sergeant looked in distaste at Geordie, who was in a horrible mess: he was snivelling miserably, and his face and shirt front were smeared with straw and blood.

'You do that, sir.'

Christine and John Murray took Geordie along the Cowgate and through the Port, until they found a wynd leading up to the Canongate beside Balmuir's house. John Murray pulled a piece of cloth from his pocket and handed it to Christine.

'Here, redd your cousin's nose for him. I doubt Balmuir never thought what this piece of linen was to be used for.'

Christine tried to mop the blood with the cloth; but Geordie's nose continued to flow. He had to walk along with his head in the air while his cousins each held an arm, as he could not see where he was going.

They had taken the least busy route they could, but unfortunately for Geordie, his whole family was at home when he was brought in.

'You young coof,' said Balmuir contemptuously. 'I'll hae you whipped for it when your neb stops blooding.'

Lady Balmuir and Elizabeth screamed, and had to be

revived with burnt feathers. Henrietta was full of envy that she had not been there to see the fight.

After the excitement had subsided, Balmuir took the Murrays to the door himself, and waved away the man-servant. He shook John Murray's hand gratefully. 'I'm much obliged to you, John. A great fool I'd look, a Lord of Session, if Geordie had been up before the magistrates!'

'I hope you'll not be too severe on him, cousin Adam,' said Christine.

The old man patted her cheek. 'If I am, it will be be-cause he hadna the smeddum to defend himself,' he re-assured her. 'I had many a bicker myself at his age, but I had the sense to jink the bailies.'

Christine smiled to herself. It was hard to imagine the portly Adam Grant as a nimble-footed schoolboy.

As he thanked them again, Murray said: 'Sir, I am glad to hae been of service.'

'I'll not forget it,' said Balmuir warmly, 'either here or in the Company offices. John, if there's anything you set your mind on, come to me.'

As they walked home, Christine saw her father's hand slide into the pocket where Ewan had thrust the letters. He turned the packet over and over, and seemed very down-cast. Already, Christine thought, he was regretting the promise he had made to Ewan.

CHAPTER ELEVEN

Death on the Stair

On Sunday morning John Murray sat on the window-seat looking down at the street. He sat there so long without moving that Christine at last went up and touched his arm.

'Is there anything ails you, father?'

His face was tight with anxiety as he turned round. 'Nothing at all,' he said, and turned back towards the street.

Christine was sure he was brooding over his arrangement with Ewan. He could not be afraid of the risk he was taking, since he had considered this before. It could only be that he disliked the thought of using Lord Balmuir to carry the letters to Perth. Perhaps he felt that he would be breaking the old man's trust in him.

Her guess was soon proved right. On Monday night, Ewan visited her father after supper. He was wearing a heavy cloak and sword. It was the first time that Christine had seen him armed.

'I've come with your money,' he announced.

John Murray showed no interest. He paced round the room, his hands twisting behind his back. Then he said abruptly: 'See here, Ewan. Do we hae to send these letters before the end of the month?'

Christine saw Ewan's eyes go hard and watchful. 'If there's a way of sending them, they must go.'

Murray looked at him unhappily. 'I'd be better pleased if we didna use Balmuir's chaise to send them. In January I expect a Company messenger will ride to Perth. Let's send them then.'

'No,' said Ewan angrily. 'They must be distributed before the roads up the glens are blocked with snow. What's the matter with you? Balmuir refused to help you with your land. It would be a pretty trick to make him our accomplice without him knowing it.'

'He has been kind to me,' said Murray indignantly. 'Thanks to him, I hae good work with the Company, and Christine here is aye about with his lassies.'

Ewan slapped his gloves against the table and laughed in an unpleasant way. 'Conscience-money, my dear John. Now, where will his chaise be on Wednesday night?'

'At the inn opposite his house in the Canongate.'

Ewan laughed at his sullen face. 'I have the best argument of all in my pocket.' He brought out a small leather bag, and pulled open the draw-string at its mouth. On to the table he counted out ten bright yellow coins.

'There you are!' he said triumphantly. 'Ten sterling guineas. No private man in Edinburgh has so much gold in his house – not even Lord Balmuir.'

Fascinated, Christine picked up one of the guineas. She had never seen a gold coin before. Even in Edinburgh, silver was scarce, and gold was never seen. The bright guinea seemed more like a jewel than money for spending.

John Murray's hands slid over the heap of coins. He went to the kitchen, and returned with the tea-caddy which they could never afford to fill, even with the cheapest Bohea. He unlocked it, and put the guineas in.

Ewan watched him with contemptuous delight. 'Take good care of them, John. If you're sensible, there will soon be other shiners to join them.'

Murray glared at the locked box as if he hated it.

Ewan tapped his arm. 'I want a private word with you.' He glanced mockingly at Christine. 'I rely on Miss Murray to keep you loyal to the old cause, but there are some things I would not like to inflict on her delicate ears.'

John Murray stood up obediently and took Ewan to his own room. He clutched the tea-caddy under his arm. They talked, in low, murmuring voices, for a long time. When they reappeared, John Murray still seemed uneasy, but Ewan was in high spirits.

'Good-bye, John,' he said. 'I'll see you in the spring, perhaps.'

Christine could not stop herself from saying: 'Are you leaving Edinburgh, Mr McDonnell?'

He turned round with the same mocking, aggressive expression he had worn when they first met. 'Yes, Miss Murray. I am sailing for France on Wednesday night, on a boat that unloaded a load of claret at Leith yesterday. I shall be back, never fear.'

After Ewan left them, John Murray sat staring into the fire. He did not move even when a coal leapt out and burned by his foot. Christine threw it back into the grate with the tongs.

'Father,' she said quietly, then louder: 'Do you hear me?'

He looked round, but his eyes were still vacant. She tried to distract him. 'Lilias has heard that Lady Strathdallin has ordered six wooden boxes. Kate up the glen says she is leaving the big house.'

Her words only irritated him. 'You should ken better than to listen to servants' clashes, Christine. Get on with your embroidery, and let me think.'

She dropped her eyes, and went back to the gay pattern of birds and leaves. She felt very depressed. She had not achieved anything by going to the cock-fight, and her boldness had only led her into a quarrel with Jamie. She had not seen him since.

She looked at her father: now he seemed more dejected than ever, despite the money Ewan had given him. He seemed to be regretting most bitterly what he had done, even if his reasons were not sensible. He was vexed about a point of honour when he should have been worrying about his safety, and what would happen to Lilias and her if he were caught. She dared not speak to him about it again:

her only hope was that he might change his mind by Wednesday night.

Yet it was so hard to keep silence! Whom could she turn to for advice?'

It was obviously impossible to say anything to Lord Balmuir or his family.

Lilias would probably scream and break out weeping if she told her.

The Lindsays? Mr Lindsay would be a staunch Whig, and would not put personal friendship before what he considered to be his duty. Mrs Lindsay would support her husband. Old Mrs Lindsay was a kind of Jacobite herself, in a romantic way, but 'she knew where her snuff came from'. She would never let herself become involved in a treasonable plot.

One name she kept until the end: Jamie. She bent to poke the fire, afraid that her father would notice her flushed cheeks. As soon as the name formed in her mind, her thoughts dissolved into confusion, her lips curved into a smile, and she could hardly sit still.

She would go to Jamie and explain her true reason for going to the cock-fight. Then he would be ashamed of his hard thoughts about her, and be anxious to help. He would think of some clever but simple scheme, and all would come right.

As soon as she had decided to do this, Christine felt immensely relieved. Her thoughts about Jamie occupied her for the rest of the evening. They were vague, but very cheerful. Even when John Murray conducted their nightly prayers, she found her mind slipping back to the same pleasant subject. When she said good-night to him, she had almost forgotten why he looked so sad.

Tuesday morning brought the coldest weather she had yet known in Edinburgh. The slush of melted snow had frozen into crusts of black ice on the street; an icy wind rattled the windows and blew the ashes out of last night's fire. It was so cold that she lit the fire in the parlour straight after breakfast, although her fingers were almost too stiff to sift the cinders. She told Lilias to pile up the kitchen fire as well, and never mind the waste.

In the bleak grey light, how foolish last night's plans seemed! How daft she had been, Christine told herself. Jamie would be horrified by her story. To involve himself with Jacobite spies – the very idea was preposterous!

The day dragged on; the parlour fire, when they managed to make it blaze up, was little comfort: the smoke and sparks were blown into the room, but most of the heat flew up the chimney. Christine cleaned and polished every room. The coal-ash would undo her work at once, but it was the only way to keep warm.

At one o'clock she went down to Lucky Robertson's shop to buy a pie for herself and Lilias. The heat of the oven was luxury after her own chilly home. She stood beside it talking to Lucky.

'I dinna ken how some folk manage in this weather without a fire-room,' said Lucky, as she rolled out her pastry. 'There's Jock Forbes up in the attic. He hasna but one fire-room and the bairns sleep in it these nights. He telt me that when he woke up this morning, he had icicles in his hair!'

'No!' exclaimed Christine in horror.

'Aye,' replied Lucky with gusto. 'Then some laddies found a dead dog in the North Loch this morn. They say the beast had gone to drink, and before he could raise his head, the ice froze solid over his neb and lugs.'

'Poor beast,' said Christine doubtfully. The story sounded far-fetched.

'Then there's his lordship up the stair. "Lord Niddrie," I cried out to him, "you'll take your death, going out on a day like this." He wouldna heed me, the silly old carl. He's away to Guffie's his lone, just as usual.'

Christine picked up the pie and left her. After they had eaten it crouched over the kitchen fire, Lilias asked if she could go out for an hour or two. She explained haltingly that she had promised to go with Donald MacLaren to the Canongate to order a pair of silver spoons.

'He says it is the custom in this country,' said Lilias, as if she had come to Africa, instead of to the southern part of her native land. 'It is a great extravagance, but I am wanting to please him.'

Christine shivered and told her she could go. She supposed that the spoons were some kind of betrothal present.

While Lilias was out she tried to write a letter to Lady Strathdallin. She made a joke of the rumours that Lilias had heard from Kate up the glen. In the middle of writing about the wooden boxes, she thought she heard an unusual noise on the stair.

She put down her pen and listened. There was a gasping cry, followed by a thud, as if someone had fallen.

Christine ran to the door and flung it open. Sprawling on his back, half on the stair and half on the landing, was Lord Niddrie. One hand clawed at his neck-cloth, and the other was feebly beating with his stick. Christine dropped on her knees and loosened his cravat. His face was blotched horribly and his eyes were rolling.

'Sir, what ails you?' she cried. 'What can I do?' Her action seemed to have brought him no relief. His mouth was quivering and his face twisted more and more violently.

Christine ran up to Lord Niddrie's flat and beat on the door. There was no reply. She ran down again past the writhing body and tirled at the Lindsays' door. 'Mrs Lindsay!' she screamed.

Jamie opened the door. She flung herself at him.

'Come quick! There's Lord Niddrie fallen on the stair, and his clerk is out.'

Jamie sprang up the steps in front of her. In the light from the open door, Lord Niddrie's face was now a dirty white in colour, streaked with red.

'I think it's his heart. I'll go for Dr Herries. He lives in the next close. Christine, bide beside him, till we come.'

Christine gulped and nodded. She wanted to fetch a blanket to put over Lord Niddrie, but was afraid to leave him. He lay more quietly now, with one hand crooked round the newel of the stair. He seemed to be unconscious. Her pity was mingled with revulsion against the grotesque, contorted features of the old man.

Soon Jamie returned with Dr Herries. The physician groped inside Lord Niddrie's silk waistcoat, then shook his head.

'I canna feel his heart at all. I'm feared he's gone. Poor soul.' He looked seriously at Jamie. Jamie said:

'There's nobody in our house but myself, and Christine says that his clerk is out.'

Christine felt a scream begin in her throat. She put her hands to her face, and harsh, noisy sobs broke from her.

'Go to your own place, lassie,' said Dr Herries in a kindly voice. 'You've had a bad shock. Jamie here will help me lift the old man up the stair.'

Christine could not bear to go into the empty flat. She watched them hoist the body and move it awkwardly round the narrow bend of the stair. Dr Herries had a look of professional detachment; Jamie compressed his lips grimly and concentrated on what he was doing. The feet and legs disappeared first round the bend of the turnpike; then Lord Niddrie's wig fell off, and the last thing Christine saw was his white, bald head bobbing up and down as Jamie supported the shoulders.

She could not stop herself crying. A door opened below, and the elder Miss Chisholm came up to her.

'Michty me, Miss Murray, whatever's happened?'

'It's Lord Niddrie,' sobbed Christine. 'He's fallen on the stair. I think he's dead. Jamie and Dr Herries have just taken him up.'

The other sister appeared and had to be told as well. They both fussed over Christine: one of them took her firmly by the arms, whispering: 'The smelling-bottle, Euphemia – and the other remedy,' while the other tiptoed downstairs with an expression both excited and shocked.

Christine, blind with tears, felt herself pulled into her own flat and pushed on to the window-seat.

'My dear lassie, what a terrible thing for you to see!' cried Miss Chisholm. Her sister rushed in with a crystal bottle which she held under Christine's nose. The sharp odour made her catch her breath and cough; at once another small silver bottle was pushed to her lips.

'Go on, sup this,' encouraged the elder Miss Chisholm. 'We keep it for medicine.' Christine swallowed a fiery mouthful of what she thought must be brandy. She spluttered, but it made her stop crying.

'Where's your tea?' asked the other sister. 'There's nothing like a dish of tea when a body's in a steer.'

'We dinna hae tea,' whispered Christine.

'Not hae any tea! Euphemia, let's down the stair and mask the pot,' said the elder. 'You bide here, Miss Murray, in your own home, and we'll bring it up to you.'

They both went out. Christine leant back exhausted against the window-sill. There was a rasp at the door, and when she did not reply, it was pushed open slowly. Jamie came in.

'How are you, Christine?' He came to sit beside her.

Christine sniffed and swallowed. 'Fine, now. I'm sorry I was such a bairn. Is he – is he really –'

'Aye, I'm feared he is,' said Jamie gently. 'Dr Herries said he must hae died as soon as the attack was over. He was a great age, Christine. The clerk is back now. He'll see to everything. Try not to be upset.'

His comforting tone brought her tears on afresh. 'I ken he was old. I'm not greeting for that. At least, I am, but not – but not – Jamie, it's the shock of it, forbye everything else.'

'Aye, I ken.' He put his arm round her in a brotherly way. If the horror of the last half-hour had not still been with her, it would have been almost pleasant to be weeping on his shoulder.

'Christine,' he said, 'I canna bear to see you taking on like this. Is there something else, besides Lord Niddrie? Can I do anything to help you? Tell me.'

She pressed her face against his coat. 'I canna. It's too fearsome.'

He gave her a gentle shake. 'Come on, tell me. I'd do anything to help you.'

She lifted her tear-streaked face. 'Would you, Jamie?' she wailed, and grasped his hands. 'I'm in sair trouble, and you're the only one who can help me. It's my father.'

'Why? Does he beat you?' He looked angry.

The misunderstanding forced a weak laugh from her. 'Na, na. He's in trouble himself, and I want to stop him.'

In a few moments the thing that had seemed so impossible had been done. She had told him everything about her father, and Ewan, and the Jacobite plot.

Jamie's face grew more and more serious. At the end he said: 'Christine, there is only one thing you can do. You must say to your father that if he persists in this daft scheme, you will go to the magistrates. This is treason.'

'I couldna!' she cried with passion. 'He really would beat me then, and I'd not stop him from sending the letters. If only I could stop the letters from going to Perth, then I'm sure he'd think better on what he's done, and come to his senses. He doesna really want to do it, I'm sure. Mr McDonnell is forcing him.'

'He has already taken Mr McDonnell's money,' pointed out Jamie. 'In the technical sense, your father's committed treason already. The *animus* is there, if not yet the *factum*.'

Christine turned on him furiously. 'Dinna use your legal cant to me! He's my father, and if you'll not help me, Jamie, I'm sorry I ever asked you.'

Jamie looked upset and bewildered. 'Christine, if there was anything I could do lawfully, I would. But I canna see what's to be done, once the letters are in the chaise.'

Christine drew her breath sharply. It was as if the terrible upheaval of Lord Niddrie's death had made her mind work twice as fast. The plan that came to her was so obvious, it was strange she had never thought of it before.

'Jamie, we can take the letters out of the chaise! All the mail is to lie there overnight. Mr McDonnell's letters will never be missed. We can wait until my father has put them in with the rest.'

Jamie drew back in horror, and snatched his hands away. '*We?*'

Christine's lips trembled. 'Can you think of a better way?'

Jamie looked wretched. 'Aye, what I said before. Go to the magistrates – or make your father think you will.'

'I'll not, I'll not!' Christine shouted at him. A memory of the cock-fight came to her. 'You're a fugie, Jamie Lindsay. You're more feared than a lassie.'

Jamie sat bolt upright, white and angry. 'Aye, I mind on it now. Yon cock-fight. If I'm a lassie, Christine Murray, you're a disnatured, unwomanly creature. It would set you fine to go melling with stable-lads for those letters. You'd scart their eyes out if they tried to stop you.'

Christine burst into tears. 'You're ungentle and a blaggart to call me such names,' she sobbed. 'I hated the cock-fight. I only went to hear what Mr McDonnell would say to my father. I was near on sick when I saw it, and Geordie's nose blooded all over my new gown. It was horrible!'

Jamie looked at her in consternation. 'Christine, my dear! I didna ken. Forgie me. I'll unsay it all.'

Timidly, she took his hands. 'I thought you were my friend. Will you not help me?'

'Christine –' he began firmly. He sighed as he looked at her eyes, still brimming with tears. 'I *canna* help you.' She stared at him silently, still clinging to his hands. 'Christine, I canna. It would be as bad as what Mr McDonnell is doing.'

'Please, please, Jamie,' she begged. 'What am I going to do? You're the only one I can ask. How can you be so unkind?'

'Christine, dinna keep on pressing me. I canna do it.' But he sounded more uncertain.

'You said you'd do anything to help me,' she reminded him. 'Nobody need see us. We'll go to the stables when it's dark. I promise not to do anything daft if there's anyone near the chaise.'

Jamie's dark eyebrows tightened in a frown. 'It would hae to be gey late on in the evening, to make sure –' He broke off with a rueful smile.

Christine tried to hide her joy. 'Hae I persuaded you?'

'So it seems,' he admitted. 'You *are* a witch,' he added in a teasing, puzzled voice, and looked at her in the way he had looked when they met on the stair over the volume of Shakespeare.

'Thank you, thank you, Jamie!' She flung her arms round him in a burst of relief and happiness, as the two Misses Chisholm came into the room bearing a tray of tea and wheaten bread.

CHAPTER TWELVE

Christmas Night

On Wednesday morning, the twenty-fifth of December, the stair of Davidson's Land was unusually quiet. The tenants went up and down as silently as they could, and the customers outside the pie-shop talked in low voices, sometimes casting a solemn look up at Lord Niddrie's windows. Jock Forbes had gone into Lord Niddrie's house, but the clerk insisted on seeing to all himself. The only thing he would accept was a bowl of hot broth that Mrs Lindsay sent up to him in the middle of the day.

Christine sat huddled over the fire with a book, thinking sadly about the dead judge, and wondering how the time would ever pass until the hour she had arranged to meet Jamie.

Henrietta called in to say good-bye until the New Year. Lady Balmuir was taking her daughters to Balmuir House for a few days, and their father would follow on Thursday afternoon. Henrietta was bubbling with excitement, although she had had a slight disappointment. Mr Patterson had not yet finished the gold necklace that had been ordered for her Christmas present.

'Maybe it will be ready in time for your father to bring it to you,' said Christine listlessly.

'Maybe he will,' said Henrietta, all smiles again. She kissed her cousin, and ran out to meet the family coach. Christine forgot her immediately, and began to think about Jamie.

Once Jamie had been persuaded to help her, he had taken charge of the arrangements. He had asked her what time her father would put the letters into the chaise, and how long it would take him to walk up from the stables to Davidson's Land.

'I'll tell my mother that I'm going down the street to see Geordie,' he had said. 'My father will be with the Greenshanks, so he'll never ken I'm out. What about you, Christine?'

She said that she would tell Lilias that she had been invited to visit Henrietta. But she insisted that she should meet Jamie before her father came home. He would probably know that her cousin had already left the Canongate. She could cover her 'mistake' somehow when she returned, but she did not think she could deceive him if she had to make the excuse to him.

Over their dinner of cheese and herrings, Lilias said: 'A strange thing was after happening yesterday. Do you mind on yon woman who came to see your father, at the beginning of December? She came late in the evening. I put my head through the door, then I went away again, for I saw your father busy talking to her.'

'You mean Mrs Patterson, the goldsmith's wife.'

'Would that be her name?' said Lilias. 'You never told me. Yesterday afternoon Donald took me to the silversmith James Gilchrist, to order those spoons I was telling you about.'

'Gilchrist!' ejaculated Christine, remembering the initials on the snuff-box. 'Go on.'

'As we were talking to the silversmith, this Mrs Patterson came in. He smiled at her, excused himself, and fetched a wee box from inside the shop. He called her "Mary", and she called him "father". Is that not strange?'

Christine smiled. 'It's not surprising her father should be a jeweller, as well as her husband.' She made a private vow that this information should never come to her father.

'Wait!' said Lilias excitedly. 'The door of the shop was open, facing on the street. Now suddenly, Mistress Patterson gied a great cry, clapped her hand to her breast – like this – and cried out: "It's he! He's come back!".'

Lilias' attempts to convey the scene were ludicrous; but behind her gaping mouth and popping eyes, Christine could imagine the shock that Mrs Patterson had received. If Lilias had reported the words correctly, they could only mean that Mrs Patterson had seen her former lover, to whom she had given the snuff-box.

'Why did she call out?' Christine asked. 'Who was in the street?'

'A great crowd of folk. She ran out of the door, but she didna get far, for she fainted on the doorstep. Her father took her behind the shop.'

When asked again, all Lilias could say was that Mrs Patterson must have seen either a red-coated officer or two young men in fine laced coats, who happened to pass at that moment.

Christine made Lilias promise not to mention the incident to her father, saying that he had been disturbed by Mrs Patterson's visit, and wanted to hear no more of her.

At a quarter to eight she left the house. In a fold of her plaid she had put the tinder-box from the kitchen and a rushlight: it might be difficult to identify the letters in the darkness. She also took her embroidery scissors, in case the letters were tied with tape or string.

She stepped cautiously through the archway on to the last few steps leading down to the pavement. The cold snatched her breath away. There was a sparkling frost, and the ice gleamed here and there on the slate roofs as the moonlight caught it. There was not such an intense blackness as on the night she had gone to meet her father at the Netherbow Port.

Christine muffled her head in her plaid; a figure slipped out of a doorway beside her. Her heart leapt into her throat, but a low whisper reassured her.

'It's me, Christine.' Jamie was wearing a long cloak and a three-cornered hat. The cloak was pulled over his ears, and his eyes gleamed at her. Christine giggled nervously.

'You look like a bogle. Let me see your face.'

He pulled the cloak down a couple of inches, then took her arm.

'Come away. Your father might see us.'

They hurried down the street, avoiding lighted doorways, and any people they met. Christine whispered that she had brought a tinder-box, and was pleased by Jamie's approval. She could feel that he was tense with excitement. His steps were uneven, and she could hardly keep pace with him.

Christine shrank back from the light as they came to the Netherbow Port. It would be terrible if they met her father coming through.

'Let me go through first,' said Jamie. 'If I see your father, I'll turn back. If I dinna appear in a few moments, come through your lone. Are you feared?'

'No,' said Christine doubtfully. Her appetite for the adventure was disappearing as Jamie's increased. All her energy had gone into persuading him to help her; now she only felt weak and terrified.

When he disappeared through the arch, she made herself count to fifty. A few men came through, but Jamie did not return. Pulling her plaid even closer, she scurried to the other side of the Port, into the safe darkness of a doorway. Almost at once Jamie was beside her. There they waited until they saw John Murray walk through the gateway, and disappear into the High Street. Christine sighed with relief. The first danger was over.

'We'll go to the stables the same way as when we met Henrietta for the pic-nic,' said Jamie.

They went under the tall arch of the Watergate, and past the horse-pond where the officers had been ducked after the riot. They trod very cautiously along the puddles and icy cobbles of the back street. Faintly, in the darkness, they could make out the row of tall doorways, arched and wide enough to let through a coach. A faint light glimmered between the top of the doors and the vaulted stone arch. Jamie groped over the surface of the first pair of doors.

'There's just a pin to hold it,' he said. 'It isna locked.'

They pressed their faces against the wood. On the other side of the door there was a confusion of small sounds: the crackling of straw, the noisy breathing of the animals, slight chinks as of metal on stone.

'I dinna think there's anyone in there,' said Jamie. He listed the hasp off the staple and pulled one door a few inches towards him. A brighter stream of light flooded through the crack. Christine peered over his shoulder.

There were two long rows of stalls for the horses. Their rumps gleamed in the light of a horn lantern suspended on the far wall. One or two of them turned their heads and blew gently down their nostrils as the door creaked. On one side of the building stood a row of coaches and chaises.

Jamie squeezed himself through the gap and Christine followed him. There was a damp, warm smell inside. They could hear shouts and singing from the inn above the stables.

'Will you ken the chaise when you see it?'

'I think so. It has red leather inside, and it's gilded round the edges of the doors.'

There were five vehicles. Two of them were heavy family coaches, and the others were carriers' waggons. But Lord Balmuir's chaise was not there.

She stood there, too wretched to move, when Jamie's hand suddenly grasped her shoulder.

'Christine, maybe the stables are full – you see there's not much room. Maybe it's standing in the inn-yard.'

Christine caught her breath in hope, as he pointed to a small door in the middle of one row of horse-stalls. 'That should let us into the yard.'

The horses stirred uneasily as they came near them, and one whinnied loudly. Jamie pulled Christine into the shadows as the horn lantern flickered in a sudden draught.

But the door remained shut: it had been only a gust of wind.

Even Jamie hesitated before the small door. 'It'll be gey mirk,' he said reassuringly. 'Nobody will see us.' He hesitated.

'They're making a din up there,' said Christine. Jamie grinned up at the unplastered roof of the stables. 'It'll be travellers from England. This is what they cry Christmas night in England. Their ministers dinna mind the celebration.' He swallowed. 'Come away, Christine. We'll hae to go outside.'

There was little danger that anyone in the inn would see them, as the door opened directly under the stair leading to the travellers' upstairs room. But someone might be out in the yard.

They slipped out quickly, then stood leaning against the wall, rigid with apprehension. The yard was deserted. The stairway and the great jutting overhang of the second storey threw their side into darkness, and there were balconies on either side of the yard. In the centre, the moon flashed back from some frozen puddles and the stone horse-trough, and the lighted windows round the yard splashed some brightness on the cobbles.

Christine tugged Jamie's arm, and pointed under one of the balconies. 'Look! Can you not see the shafts sticking out?'

They flattened themselves against the shadow of the wall and slowly edged round, always keeping their backs pressed against the rough stone. Once they were startled by someone clattering down the steps. He rushed to the horse-trough, broke the ice, and splashed water over his face. Then he ran indoors again.

'Ower much claret,' said Jamie, with a grim chuckle.

The chaise was Lord Balmuir's. They unlatched a door and groped inside. Christine's hand met rough sacking tied round three or four very bulky parcels.

'We'll hae to strike the light.'

'Not yet,' hissed Jamie. 'Let's try without, first.'

Christine remembered the small compartment under the seat where she had put her bundle of clothes when she first came to Edinburgh. She undid the catch, and the board fell down. Inside she felt a smooth leather packet.

'I think I hae it,' she said. She turned the packet over in her fingers, and felt the stitching. 'Aye, I'm sure of it.' Suddenly she felt frightened and longed to run away.

'Let's go, Jamie,' she begged. 'I'm feared someone will come.'

They slid to the ground and shut the door of the chaise behind them. As they turned towards the yard, they saw a man facing them. He stood quite still in the brightest patch of moonlight, muffled in a cloak, with a travelling-bag in his hand. It was Ewan.

Christine went chill with horror. Wordlessly she pointed out the figure to Jamie. He stiffened. It was uncanny, the way that Ewan stood there without the slightest movement.

Jamie's lips touched her ear. He mouthed the words: 'I'm not sure he's really seen us. Bide a wee.'

For some moments the strange game went on. Then Ewan put the cloak-bag on the ground and, very slowly, came towards them. He must have heard them moving in the chaise, Christine thought. Perhaps he had come to make sure her father really had put his letters with the rest of the mail. But surely he knew that they could see him, standing there in the moonlight?

Then suddenly she realized what had happened. Ewan suspected that someone was tampering with the chaise, although he could not see them. But he dared not make a noise; he dared not show too much interest. If there were a scuffle, people might rush out of the inn to see what was going on.

Jamie seemed to realize this too. Once more he spoke close to her ear. 'Run out of the yard and meet me by the Netherbow Port. I'll keep his eyes fixed here. He'll not dare to make a hurly-burly, and I'll soon jink him.'

'I canna leave you!'

'Take the letters with you.' Jamie pushed her firmly away.

Christine slid into the darkest corner behind the chaise. She could not leave Jamie to face Ewan alone. She bit her knuckles in an agony of fear.

A thin strip of silver suddenly flashed along Ewan's cloak. He had drawn his sword and was weaving its point gently round and round as he stepped towards the chaise. Christine thought of the cock-fight. But none of the birds had had the silent, evil intensity of Ewan.

'Dinna let him hurt Jamie!' she prayed fiercely to herself. 'Dinna let him find him!' She thrust the letters into the bodice of her gown and scrabbled over the cobbles with her finger-nails for some weapon. She found half of a broken jug, and raised it above her head.

Before she could throw it Ewan leapt into the darkness under the balcony. She heard the sword scrape against something, then a sharp cry. There was a heavy thump; two bodies rolled over and over, half in the shadow, and a foot kicked the sword into the middle of the yard. It tinkled across the cobbles and lay by the horse-trough.

Then something miraculous happened. The door of the inn opened, and a horde of men poured on to the stairs, singing, with tankards in their hands. They tumbled in a merry, jostling crowd down to the yard, and surged straight towards the chaise. Christine saw a huddled shape seem to rise out of the cobbles, and stumble in a strange, crab-like fashion towards the cloak-bag and sword. Still bent almost double, Ewan ran into the street.

The merrymakers swayed round the pillars under the balcony, supporting each other, and shouting out noisy toasts. Then they all crowded round the horse-trough and began to sing a Christmas carol.

'Jamie!' shouted Christine, throwing herself towards the chaise. 'Are you all right?'

He leant against the wall with his hands to his face. 'I dinna ken,' he muttered.

'Let me see.' Gently she pulled his hands away. The scandalized tenants of the yard had flung their windows open, and the streaming light now reached even under the balconies. There was a jagged scratch from his eye to his chin. It did not look very deep, but it was bleeding badly.

'He's hurt you!' she said, in a breaking voice.

'Aye, and I hurt him,' replied Jamie with satisfaction. 'I gied him a bonny dunt on the shins.'

There was a large bruise on his forehead. Christine found herself choked with tears. It was daft, she told herself furiously, to cry now the danger was past. 'Jamie, Jamie,' she sobbed, 'he might hae killed you!'

Jamie's arms went round her, then his lips were near her face again, and he kissed her. Christine clung to him, laughing and crying at the same time; a strange new delight danced through her, and the frosty air felt as if it were bright with fire.

Jamie's voice was husky. 'Christine, my love, what are we going to do with the letters?'

Christine brought her mind back to practical matters. The noisy yard was now thronged with people.

'Let's burn them,' she said decisively. 'Right here. I dinna want to ken what's in them.'

They dropped on their knees beside the chaise, and Christine struck the flint. After a few moments of patient effort, the tinder caught, and she blew up a small flame. Jamie's eyes met hers across it, dark and glowing. She smiled; then held the first letter to the tiny flame. She fed them one by one to the blaze, until they were all consumed.

Someone in the crowd noticed them and raised a shout. He probably thought they were trying to set fire to the chaise. The man came stumbling towards them, but they were too quick for him. They leapt to their feet and ran hand-in-hand into the Canongate.

So long as Jamie's arm was round her, Christine felt happy and exultant. They had stolen the letters and her father was safe. It was a pity that Ewan had interrupted them, but they had outwitted him, and the Jacobite letters would not now travel in Lord Balmuir's chaise.

When they passed through the light cast from a window she could see the streak of blood on Jamie's face. It made her want to cry again, but she felt proud and triumphant as well, as if he had been fighting to save her, and not the letters, from Ewan.

When they reached Davidson's Land, they stood and faced each other, although it was too dark to see.

'Well, Christine, I'll call on you in the morning,' said Jamie.

His tone echoed the flatness inside her. They would have to leave each other now, and go back to their respective families. It seemed all out of joint, she thought, when they had gone through so much together. She took his arm impulsively, then drew back, with hot cheeks, in case he thought she was asking him to kiss her again.

'Will you be all right, with your father?' he asked anxiously.

'Och, never fear,' she said with pretended cheerfulness. With a sinking heart she went up the stair alone.

Her father did not question the reason she had given Lilias for going out so late. He was preoccupied with the letter he was reading.

'Look at this, Christine,' he said at last.

The letter merely said that Lady Strathdallin was leaving Perthshire, and would come to live in Edinburgh in the spring. She could say no more at present: but John Murray should be told the rest in the New Year.

'It isna like Isobel at all,' he said, 'to make a mystery yon way. There's something wrong. I'm gey worried about her.'

It was the first time that Christine had ever heard her father call Lady Strathdallin by any other name than her territorial title.

'Would you credit it,' he went on, 'this was lying in the

post-office for me this forenoon, but I've been so busy all day, I've not had time to break the seal.'

'And you've not had time to eat either, I suppose,' she said. 'I'll away to get you some supper.'

He gave her a grateful look, and drank the broth which she carried into the room for him. As they talked over the strange news, he seemed to become less anxious. It began to dawn on Christine that her father had a much stronger affection for Mrs Murray of Strathdallin than she had ever realized.

She did not know how much later it was when Ewan tirled at the door. Christine's mouth went dry with fear, and she looked away as he entered.

There was an angry slap as Ewan flung his gloves and hat on to the table. Christine noticed that one of his stockings was torn. His ugly face was twisted with rage. He did not try to explain his abrupt entry. 'A fine pickle you've made of our business, haven't you?'

Murray frowned. 'What the deil are you havering about?'

Ewan almost snarled: 'The letters are not in Lord Balmuir's chaise.'

'Of course they are. Hae you been spying to see that I earned my fee?' He looked contemptuously at Ewan.

A tight smile split across Ewan's face. 'You may recall, my dear Mr Murray, that I have been putting up at the inn where Balmuir's chaise is kept. As I walked across the yard, intending to set out for Leith, I happened to see the chaise standing there.'

John Murray grunted. 'Aye, and you wondered if I'd played you false. You can spare your trouble. The letters are in the small compartment under the seat. Are you satisfied?'

Ewan was well in control of himself now. He sat down and gently flicked his sleeve-ruffles into order. Christine began to panic. How long could she keep her secret? Sweat pricked on her forehead.

'There was someone by the chaise, John.'

'An ostler, I suppose. What of it?'

'John,' said Ewan softly, 'either you did not put the letters in at all, or you sent someone to remove them after you had put them into the chaise. You see, after the ostler, as you call him, had gone away, and some other fellows roistering in the yard, I searched the chaise most thoroughly. The door of the compartment was open, and *the letters are not there.*'

Murray began to look uneasy. He went pale and his fingers gripped the pewter salt-cellar. He said hoarsely: 'I swear I'm telling the truth, Ewan. I did put the letters in!'

'All right,' said Ewan. 'Then who has taken them out of the chaise?'

Christine did not dare to speak a word. She wondered why Ewan had not mentioned the fight. He was watching her father intently, as if not yet sure whether he could believe him.

'He was no stable-hand, I can tell you that. He had lace at his neck. I wish I had choked him with it!'

Murray swung round with relief on his face. 'That would be it! Balmuir's footmen – they're spruce young birkies. He has two of them. Maybe Balmuir had left something in the chaise. He'd hae sent a footman ower to fetch it.' His face suddenly went pale, as he realized the implications of what he had said.

'No doubt,' said Ewan, smiling ironically at the sick look of fear in Murray's eyes. 'No doubt he found the letters as well.'

Murray shouted: 'Why did you make me do it? I told you it wasna wise to use his chaise!' He brought the tea-caddy from his bedroom, and unlocked it with shaking fingers. 'Here!' He pulled out the ten gold pieces, and the first bundle of coins and notes that Ewan had given him. 'Take them back, I dinna want them.' He threw himself despairingly into a chair by the fire.

Ewan scooped up the money, and eyed him sardonically. 'You can't buy yourself out of this trauchle, John.' The Scots word sounded odd on his lips. 'Now let me see.' He thought over the problem, smiling to himself, while John Murray watched him in rage, and hope, and fear: the whole adding up to an expression that filled Christine with loathing for Ewan, because he took away her father's dignity and made her feel ashamed of him.

Ewan's face cleared. 'I shall go to Lord Balmuir and say that the groom may have put some of my luggage in his chaise by mistake. In fact, I shall go at once, before the packet is opened.'

Murray gaped at his boldness. 'What if they have opened the letters already?'

Ewan shrugged. 'Unlikely. If they have, they cannot stop me from running out of the house, and I shall be aboard the ship and out of Leith harbour by midnight. I must arrange for someone else to handle the correspondence, John. You have failed me badly.'

There was menace in his voice.

Murray stood looking wildly at the shut door after Ewan left.

Christine fought down the waves of panic that confused her, and tried to decide what she ought to do. She did not believe that Ewan really thought the letters were unopened; and if he thought he had fought one of the servants, the last thing he would do would be to present himself at the judge's door with such a story. No: he must be going down there to throw the blame on her father. Whatever happened, she had to stop Ewan going to Lord Balmuir.

'Father,' she whispered, 'he'll not find the letters with Lord Balmuir. Jamie and I took them, and we burnt them.' Her legs collapsed under her, and she fell back in the chair in a way that would have been ludicrous at another time.

'You *what*?' The quiet tone was ten times more frightening than if he had shouted at her. His face changed from the pallor of fear to a blotched, bright red.

'He saw Jamie, and they had a fight. He canna mean only to go to Balmuir as he says. He means to do something terrible to you, father. You must stop him.'

He did not take in what she was saying. He was still struggling with the shock of what she had told him, and his anger began to boil up. He grasped her shoulders.

'You meddlesome besom, what call had you to push yourself into my affairs?' he shouted. 'See what you've done to me!' He picked up his walking-stick.

Christine backed away, throwing out her arms to protect herself. 'Father, dinna touch me!' she screamed. 'I did it to help you. I dinna want you to go to prison again for the Jacobites!'

'I'll teach you!' he shouted as he drove her into a corner. 'You and your bonny wee jo down the stair as well. I should hae kent it. Stravaiging at this hour of the night with a laddie! You were prinking yourself for Captain Binning the first night you stepped out of the house. Come here, and I'll thrash you till you screech!'

Christine crouched in the corner by the door; she sobbed with fear and indignation. She felt her father's hand heavy on her shoulder and the swish of the upraised stick. She gave a last despairing wail and waited for the blow. It never came. She looked up and saw her father throw the stick disgustedly away.

'Ach,' he said bitterly, 'you well deserve a thrashing, but I canna do it. What's the use, when the harm's done? Forbye, I well ken what a fool I've been. I've brought it on myself.'

He showed no remorse for what he had said or the fright he had given her. Christine burned with anger at his accusations; but there were more urgent matters to see to now. She tried again to explain why she thought Ewan had lied about his purpose in going to Balmuir. This time her father listened, his face dark with suspicion.

But he said he would not go after Ewan. 'Christine, I canna tell Balmuir that you burned the letters. I canna put the blame on you, though well you deserve it.' It was almost as if he wanted to be punished for his foolish behaviour.

She laid her hand defiantly on the door latch. 'Then I'll tell him myself. Come quickly now, or I'm away out.'

He saw that she meant what she said. 'All right,' he said. 'I shall come if you promise me one thing. If this ploy has reached cousin Adam already, there's an end to it as far as you're concerned. Leave me to redd the matter myself. Do you understand?' he demanded sternly.

With this partial promise, Christine had to be content.

CHAPTER THIRTEEN

The Last Set

CHRISTINE stumbled as they walked down the dark street. She was very tired, but she had no idea what time it was. Then ten struck from St Giles, and they heard the steady drum-beat of the Town Guard working their way up from the Mercat Cross. The taverns disgorged an irregular trickle of customers, and the crowd pressed them against the wall.

'Hold well out,' her father warned her, and pulled her into the middle of the street. Dozens of windows were flung open, then filth and garbage splashed down in a stinking shower that was inaccurately aimed at the gutter. Christine coughed at the sudden stench, which had only reached her from a distance before.

She tugged her father on urgently. But his footsteps dragged as if all the spirit had gone out of him. They both knew that there was little hope of overtaking Ewan before he saw Lord Balmuir. She realized despairingly that he had come out only to please her.

'What a dolt I've been,' he muttered to himself, 'what a dolt!'

Still she pulled him on, hoping that there would be something she could say to Balmuir, something that would retrieve the situation.

They came to the iron gateway of Crathie's Court. The paved courtyard inside was lit by the horn lanterns that hung over the doorways of the three houses into which the building was divided.

John Murray stepped through and looked up at Balmuir's shuttered windows. Christine shivered and felt the mettle go out of her. What lies was Ewan already telling about her father?

As he raised his hand to tirl, she pulled at his sleeve.

'Let me say I've lost one of my mother's silver rings when I came to visit my cousins. They'll hae to let me search the room, and that will gie you some time to face Balmuir. You can see what Mr McDonnell has said to him.'

He father nodded, and pulled the door-ring up and down. A man-servant opened the door, looking very surprised. He was carrying a pot of boot-wax in his hand.

'We werena expecting anymore visitors this evening, Mr Murray,' he said forbiddingly. 'What's your will?'

Christine spoke up boldly. 'I think I hae dropped a ring in my cousins' room. May I cast around for it?'

He led the way upstairs. 'Aye, but you'll hae to do it your lone, for all the servant-lassies are away with Lady Balmuir, and I dinna touch the bedrooms.'

At the head of the stair they heard voices behind a closed door. The servant pointed along the corridor. 'There's the room.'

Lord Balmuir opened the closed door.

'Why, cousin John,' he exclaimed.

'Aye, cousin Adam, it's me,' said John Murray coolly. He seemed to have recovered his firmness. Balmuir rocked to and fro on his heels with a strange look on his face. 'Come away in.'

He waved them through before him, and Christine saw Ewan sitting very much at his ease, beside the fire. He sprang up with a look of consternation, but he did not seem as alarmed as Christine had expected. From the bottle and glasses on the table beside him, he might have been an old friend come to spend the evening.

The room seemed to be some kind of study. It was small and darkly panelled, and the walls were mostly hidden by shelves of books. Balmuir's court gown was thrown over the back of a chair.

Balmuir rubbed his hands. 'Panel and pursuer both

present, and I'd be blyth if all my witnesses came to court so promptly. Sit you down again, Mr McDonnell, and you too, Christine and cousin John.' He seemed to be enjoying some grim private joke. Christine was frightened by the casual way in which Ewan lolled back in his chair and stretched his feet to the fire. Surely he had as much to fear as her father?

'Balmuir, I can see that you've been told the whole ploy. I ken I've been a fool, and I've not come to beg myself off. But I took the rue as soon as the business was arranged.' He fell silent, and scowled into the fire.

Balmuir nodded gravely to himself, and turned to Ewan. 'Mr McDonnell, what do you say to that?'

Ewan smiled. 'Obviously, he will excuse himself.'

'And you,' rumbled Balmuir warningly. Ewan bowed his head stiffly.

'As you say, sir. It was foolish, I acknowledge, but one cannot be too nice over methods when one serves one's country in this way.'

Balmuir made a gesture of disgust, but said nothing.

To Christine, the conversation seemed senseless. Her father glared in bewilderment, clenching his fists. 'What the deil are you playing at?' he demanded of Ewan.

'Cousin John,' said Balmuir, 'you hae been sadly glaikit by this ingenious gentleman, although in a good cause. Since you seem to be a reluctant Jacobite, you should not take it hard. Mr McDonnell is a spy for our Government, although he is thought by the Jacobites to be one of their own men.'

Ewan smiled at the astonished faces of Christine and her father. At once the inconsistencies of his behaviour made sense; his apparent recklessness was nothing of the sort: he knew that he had nothing to fear. His behaviour at the riot had been an elaborate pretence.

'So now you know my true business,' said Ewan with complacency.

'Aye,' said Balmuir steadily, 'and a dirty one it is, too.'

Ewan flushed. 'You are well content to profit from it, sir. We are not concerned with what you think of me.'

'That's true,' agreed Balmuir. 'We're here to find what became of the letters you so imprudently lost between you. Troth, it goes against my will to help you find them. Some of those silly bodies in the north will put enough on paper to hang them, though they mean nothing by it.'

Christine gulped. It was good to know that her action had been of some use after all. 'I burnt the letters,' she said.

She barely saw her father's vexed look before Ewan's fingers dug painfully into her shoulders. He shook her violently. 'You little hellcat!' he shouted angrily. John Murray pulled him away.

'Leave my lassie alone. You can settle accounts with me, Ewan.'

Ewan straightened himself, and the fury in his eyes changed to a cold gleam of hatred. 'Indeed I will. You do not seem to realize that I have told Lord Balmuir you came back here to work for the Jacobites. You opened your mouth too wide the first night I went with you to Guffie's tavern. You remember the Oak Medal you showed me? Lord Balmuir, he cannot deny that he has it in his house. John, I am sincerely glad you are not on our side. You would blab our business after one bottle of claret.'

Christine listened in horrer, as the cool voice went on and on, twisting the truth into a plausible lie.

'It isna true!' shouted John Murray. 'You sought me out to do my spying – I had no truck with the Jacobites before!'

Ewan leaned back and brought out his snuff-box. He prodded the mixture with fussy nicety. 'Confound it,' he frowned, feeling through his pockets, 'I have lost my sifting spoon.' He looked up at Murray with an evil smile. 'Can you prove what you say?'

'No, as fine you ken,' replied Murray bitterly. 'But you are a lying deil.'

Ewan took his snuff delicately. 'Ah,' he said thoughtfully. 'Well, there you are.'

Christine looked beseechingly at Lord Balmuir, who sat in silence while the two men faced and hated each other across the mahogany table. His massive face was quite still, as if he were listening to evidence in court. He looked tired and old. Christine thought of Lord Niddrie, and shivered. Surely Lord Balmuir could not believe Ewan's lies so easily?

Ewan closed his snuff-box with a click. 'My lord, whatever Mr Murray says, it is evident that he has treasonable intentions. It would be wise, I think, to remove him from the Company's employment.'

Murray's face went white. 'Do you believe him, Balmuir?'

Balmuir sighed, and stirred a little in his chair. 'I havena said so. Besides, Mr McDonnell, who are you to tell the Company whom it may employ?'

Ewan smiled viciously. 'You are a Lord of Session and very powerful in this city, sir. But the Ministers who employ me are even more important. They would be interested to hear that you kept a convicted Jacobite in your service.'

Balmuir seemed to make a decision. He heaved himself out of the chair and began to rummage among the papers on his desk. 'Here it is,' he said. He came back to the fire and settled himself comfortably before he spoke again. He held up a piece of paper.

'I am a better Whig than anyone in this room, Mr McDonnell. I dinna like your trade, sir, and I've not much notion of yourself, since your last remark. Still, it's not my affair to question the methods of our Government.' His huge body became full of wrath as he leant forward. 'Mr McDonnell, they tell me you've been meeting the Lord Justice-Clerk. This week he passed me a paper which was sent to him by one of our Government agents in France – a certain Alexander Ramsay. It's a letter you wrote to Mr

Ramsay last month. Here it is. The contents are peculiar, Mr McDonnell.'

Ewan shrugged. 'What of it? As a false spy for the Pretender, I write many letters that are not what they seem.'

Balmuir tapped the arm of his chair. 'This one has the smell of something more. You seem to be taking gold from both sides, and gieing satisfaction to neither.'

Christine saw fear leap into Ewan's eyes. 'I do not recall the letter,' he blustered.

'You'll surely not deny your own signature? It's dated from Boulogne, 4th November last. It seems you thought that Mr Ramsay was the same breed as yourself. You'd hae drawn him into your own game, if you could. But he's an honest spy for our Government – if there's any such creature. This letter's enough to hang you, man.'

'You are insulting, sir,' blazed Ewan. 'You cannot prove it.'

Balmuir waved the letter in the air. 'Then if I misjudge you, you'll not mind my sending it to your Ministers in London.'

'Give me that letter, my lord.' Ewan advanced with impatient fingers. 'Give it to me – or must I make you?'

Balmuir and Ewan stood facing each other; Christine could not believe that even Ewan would dare to use force, and Balmuir seemed to think so too. Ewan hesitated.

The tension was broken by a knock at the door. The man-servant, still holding his pot of boot-wax, put his head round the edge.

'Sir, there's another of them, a woman this time.'

'Who is it?' asked Balmuir irritably.

'Mistress Patterson, with apologies for crying in so late. She's come in a chair. Her husband's sick and couldna come himself. She has the two necklaces you ordered.'

Lord Balmuir's face softened. 'That's fine. Tell her to –' He hesitated and looked round the room.

Christine realized his difficulty. Mrs Patterson could not be dismissed from the door like a caddy. She would have expected a few words of thanks from Lady Balmuir in person, if her ladyship had been in the house. He did not want to bring her up to the study; on the other hand, the rest of the house was sheeted and fireless. He sighed as he looked down at his gouty foot. After walking a few hobbling steps to the door, he turned back.

'Dod, I canna manage that stair. She'll hae to come in here. Rab, tell her my wife isna here – you ken what to say.' The servant grinned and disappeared. Balmuir turned to his three guests.

'I'll hae to see these trinkets for the lassies. My wife would be black-affrontit if I turned her off without a thank-you.'

Ewan bowed stiffly; his eyes remained on the letter in Balmuir's hand. Christine wondered if Mrs Patterson would be embarrassed when she saw her father.

The goldsmith's wife hardly seemed to be the same person. She wore a silk gown surmounted by a fur-lined cape, and a modishly trimmed hat. She had two small leather boxes in her hands, which she smilingly held up to Lord Balmuir as she curtsied to him on the threshold.

Christine heard Ewan utter a soft, startled oath, and he turned abruptly to face the fire.

'Dinna mind my company, Mrs Patterson,' said Lord Balmuir. 'Let's hae your bonny gee-gaws on the table.'

Mrs Patterson began to cross the room. Suddenly, the jewel cases fell from her hands. She clutched the edge of a book-case, her eyes dark and brilliant in her dead-white face.

'Ewan,' she whispered in a shocked voice.

Ewan turned round and faced her warily. 'Madam?'

Mrs Patterson's face coloured again, and then crumpled into a quivering mass of grief. 'Ewan, Ewan, I canna be so changed as that.'

Ewan leaned negligently against the fireplace. 'You are mistaken, madam. We have never met before.'

The drooping figure that clung to the book-case stiffened

with anger. 'You are a wicked man, Ewan McDonnell. You mind on me well enough, and the snuff-box I gied you, and all the false things you said to me in the winter of forty-five.'

Christine heard her father's breath hiss beside her. 'Ah, so it was *you*, then – Ewan, you sent me to the hulks, and betrayed me to the soldiers at Fort Augustus!'

Ewan swung round, startled. 'Maybe this will remind you!' cried John Murray. As he lifted his arm the ruffles fell back from the red scar on his wrist. The silver snuff-box flashed as he hurled it at Ewan's face.

Ewan ducked with a growl of rage. The box crashed against the wall, then fell at Ewan's feet.

'Sirs, sirs,' called out Balmuir, 'will you cast out under my roof? Do your brawling outside.'

Ewan stooped to pick up the snuff-box. He held it in his palm for a long time; he looked at John Murray, then at Mrs Patterson, then back at John Murray again.

'So,' he said softly. There was absolute silence in the room except for the crackling of the fire. Christine felt a shiver of fear ripple down her back. She could not lift her hand from the chair she was resting it on, and her lips felt clamped together. Mrs Patterson forgot her grief and stared at Ewan in wide-eyed fear.

'So,' repeated Ewan. The sweat glistened on John Murray's forehead. Ewan's hand went to his sword-hilt and the blade flashed out. He began to step backwards towards Balmuir, but his eyes stayed fixed on Murray. He shook his left hand impatiently in the old man's face.

'Give me that paper, my lord,' he said over his shoulder. 'Quickly.'

'Get out of my house this instant, you sneck-drawing loon, or I'll hae the Guard on you!'

Ewan roughly pushed Balmuir into the chair over which he had flung his court gown. The old man went down like a barrel and glared in rage as Ewan pressed his sword-point into his ample waist-band.

'Ewan, dinna be a fool!' shrieked Mrs Patterson.

Christine turned imploringly to her father. 'Stop him, please!'

John Murray flung himself across the room and threw his arms round Ewan's waist to drag him off Balmuir. Ewan drove his elbow into Murray's stomach, just as the other man hooked his leg round his shin as he had done to the schoolboy at the cock-fight. Christine looked round for some weapon. She seized a candlestick and rushed to the fight, waiting for a chance to thrust the hot wax into Ewan's face.

Lord Balmuir tried to pull himself to his feet. He was dark red with rage, and bellowed at both the men. Then Ewan wrenched his sword-arm free, and whether by accident or on purpose the blade was driven into Balmuir's shoulder.

The old man groaned and fell back in the chair. Christine bent over him. His coat was a little torn; but although he lay back gasping, he did not seem badly hurt.

'Christine,' panted John Murray, 'run for the Town Guard!'

'I'll not leave you!' she cried, and circled round again for a chance to thrust the candle-flame where it would hurt.

At the same moment her father tripped Ewan, who sprawled on the floor at Balmuir's feet. The sword jumped out of his hand into the fireplace. Murray picked up the weapon from the hot ash, and pinned Ewan down with his foot. Ewan's lips snarled back over his teeth like a dog's; a high, thin scream came from Mrs Patterson.

With the hatred of six years glaring in his eyes, Murray exultantly dipped the sword-point towards Ewan's throat. Ewan clutched his face with both hands.

'Dinna do it,' whispered Christine. She had no pity for the ugly, twisting form that whimpered on the floor; she would almost have been glad to see him drown or break his neck; but stronger than her own hatred was the thought of the terrible guilt that would poison both their lives if her father killed the helpless man at his feet.

She ran forward and clutched her father's arm. 'Let him be!' she screamed. Murray's eyes were glazed and unseeing, as if his passion had made him drunk.

'Think – think what you're doing,' she begged him. The sword-point wavered. Her father closed his eyes, and his mouth twisted as if in pain.

'Why did you hae to speak?' he muttered. 'I could hae killed him then . . . and now I canna.'

He lifted his foot off Ewan's back and kicked him. 'Rise to your feet,' he ordered. Ewan backed towards the door.

'I'll let you go,' said Murray bitterly. 'But one thing first.' He dropped the sword and strode forward to grasp Ewan's lace cravat in his left hand. His right fist came back and he drove the knuckles into Ewan's mouth. 'Dinna bide long enough to spit out the blood,' he said roughly ,'or I'll gie you another.'

Christine gasped at the brutal words. Ewan nursed his broken lips, hardly seeming to believe that Murray would not use the sword on him.

'Get out,' shouted John Murray.

Ewan's groping hand found the door. With one quick movement he was out of the room. They heard him run down the stair.

Murray turned to Mrs Patterson, who was crouched in a corner of the room. 'You'd best be getting home,' he said.

Mrs Patterson gathered her mantle about her. 'My chair will hae gone by now. I'll not go up the street my lone. He might be biding up the close for me.'

John Murray laughed. He sounded carefree and almost happy. His eyes sparkled, and he looked many years younger. 'Dinna be feared, madam. Yon bogle will never scare any of us again. He'll be down to his ship at Leith as fast as his shanks can carry him.'

'What about Lord Balmuir?' said Mrs Patterson.

The three of them gathered about the old judge. The

wound which had seemed so slight now appeared more serious. A dark patch of blood was spreading across his coat; his mouth gaped open, and he was unconscious.

Christine ran downstairs for the servant. When she explained what had happened, he took some hot water off the fire and told her to tear up an old sheet covering the furniture in one of the unused rooms.

When they went up to the study, Mrs Patterson and John Murray had eased off Balmuir's coat and waistcoat.

'A bonny sight this is,' said the servant angrily, as he pushed them aside. 'You should think black shame on yourselves, letting an old carl like him meddle with sword-fighting.'

He scolded them without ceasing as he attended to the wound.

'How will you send word to Lady Balmuir?' asked Christine.

He looked at her as if she had been responsible for the whole incident. 'Guid kens. How can I leave him his lone?'

'She shall hear of it tonight,' said John Murray. 'Dinna fash yourself. We shall get a message to her, if I hae to walk the whole road to tell her. Let us help you lift him to his bed now.'

The huge, inert body was tremendously heavy. It took four of them to lift him in the chair and carry him to his bedroom. On a small inlaid table by the bed-curtains, Christine saw a miniature of Henrietta. For the first time, she realized that the wounding of Lord Balmuir was the worst thing that had happened during the whole, crowded night.

'We must send Dr Herries down,' she said to her father.

'Aye,' he agreed. He grasped Christine's hand. 'Dinna be feared, Christine. I saw worse on the battle-field. He'll win through.'

But she did not know if he were saying this to comfort her.

They went back to the study to retrieve Ewan's sword. Christine saw the remains of the snuff-box lying on the floor. It had been crushed flat in the struggle. She picked it up, and saw that the inscription had been obliterated except for the letters 'true. M.G.' With a furtive movement, so that the two others should not see her, she threw it into the fire.

Mrs Patterson picked up the two necklace-cases.

'What shall I do with these?' she asked helplessly.

'Let's put them on his desk – and this letter too,' said John Murray. He tried to clear a space on the desk so that the three objects would catch the eye of the first person who entered the room. He bent over the papers on the desk for a long time.

'Are you coming, then?' asked Mrs Patterson with some impatience. She was composed again, and, Christine thought, longing to tell her husband the whole terrible story. Or perhaps not quite the whole.

'Christine,' said John Murray in a choked voice, 'come here.'

His finger jabbed at a document as she looked over his shoulder. The sentences were a blur, but in larger letters than the rest, one word on it stood out: STRATHDALLIN. A few phrases danced into place: '... leased to Adam Grant ... space of Nineteen Years ... commonly known as STRATHDALLIN, from the western bank of the River Dallin to ...' The lease was signed by several names, all under the heading of 'The Commissioners for the Forfeited Estates.'

'This too is a bonny sight,' her father quoted ironically. Christine stared incredulously at the document. 'Does this mean that Lord Balmuir has leased Strathdallin for himself?'

'What else?' Her father glanced quickly at Mrs Patterson's impatient figure in the doorway. 'No wonder he is so anxious to hae the Linen Company men about the place! All those rumours you heard from your Kate up the glen,

Christine – they're true. And he is turning Isobel Murray out of her house.'

'There must be some explanation, father. He wouldna do such a thing.'

'Here it is, on paper! How can you go past that? Oh, Christine, Christine, is there to be no end to our trauchle?'

'Wheesht, now,' said Christine gently, 'we'll think on this in the morning. Let's away home now.'

He let her pull him to the door, where Mrs Patterson shrilly demanded whether she would have to wait for them all night. Christine's feet dragged with weariness. It seemed a year ago since she had walked down the street with Jamie.

CHAPTER FOURTEEN

The Reel Ends

THE next few days were worse than Christine could ever have imagined. She slept little during the night, waking several times to hear voices on the other side of the curtain. The stair door opened and shut twice, and once she heard the sound of horses' hooves clattering in the street outside. Confusedly, she thought she recognized the voice of Dr Herries.

It seemed that she had hardly shut her eyes after hearing him, when there was a loud rasping at the door. It went on and on, and she struggled awake to find her room still in darkness. There was no time to change her nightshift for her petticoat and gown, so she pulled the plaid round her shoulders and went across the parlour in her bare feet. The frenzied rasping continued until the very moment she lifted the latch.

Outside stood Lady Balmuir. She was so still, and her face such a frozen mask, that Christine could not believe she had made the agitated noise. But her hand was still uplifted to the door-ring; and the footman escorting her with a lantern stood well back at the turn of the stair.

'I wish to speak with your father,' said Lady Balmuir in her cold, precise voice.

Christine stood back without a word; Lady Balmuir's silks and furs swished across the parlour floor. As she sat down, casting a look at the chill grey ashes in the fireplace, John Murray entered. He was dressed, but wigless, his head still swathed in a night-cap. He apologized, and turned back to his room.

'Sir, do not be so ceremonious!' Lady Balmuir shrilled. 'Only tell me what happened. There is no one in our Canongate house who can tell me.'

'How is he?' asked John Murray anxiously.

Christine was surprised to see Lady Balmuir's lips tremble, and realized that she had been unjust to her. She was very upset.

'He is weak. He has bled during the night. He is not a young man, is he? But Dr Herries thinks he will recover in time.'

'Thank Heaven!' cried Murray. He began to tell her what had happened.

Christine went to the kitchen, glad that she still had some of the tea the Misses Chisholm had presented to her. She had nothing in which to offer it, except some wooden quaichs; no doubt Lady Balmuir was too agitated to notice that the Murrays had no tea-cups. She roused the startled Lilias, then raked over the kitchen embers and hung the kettle above them. She heard her father explain how Ewan had tried to seize a letter which could be used against him; how in the struggle over Ewan's sword, the point had gone into Lord Balmuir's shoulder. Most of the story her father held back.

As Christine returned to the parlour, she was amazed to see Lady Balmuir seize her father's hands and kiss them.

'Sir, you saved his life. I am sadly confused, as you see, but when my husband is out of danger, I shall try to thank you. He shall know what you have done.'

'No!' cried Murray vehemently. 'It is not true. I only —' He stopped; Christine realized that Lady Balmuir's words were like gall in his mouth: he blamed himself for causing Ewan to go to Balmuir in the first place, but he could not tell her why.

Lady Balmuir took the tea from Christine. She became composed again, and drank as if the cups had been of Sèvres porcelain, although the tea in fact tasted obnoxious in the wooden beakers.

Lady Balmuir had evidently been told the false excuse that Christine had made when she and her father went to Balmuir's house on the previous night. 'I will see that the maid searches diligently for your ring, my dear,' she said, with something of her usual composure. Then she began to talk about Ewan.

'I cannot understand why he should go to my husband, at all, and so late in the evening. Adam hates spies – even those that work for our own Government. He has often said he would rather hang one spy than a dozen horse-thieves. What business could he have with such a creature?'

John Murray winced and went red, although Lady Balmuir could have no idea how her words went home. 'I canna think, madam,' he muttered, turning away his face.

When Lady Balmuir had gone back to the Canongate, they had an early breakfast, which they ate in unhappy silence. Lilias was cross because her night had been so disturbed. She banged the dishes and fiercely hummed a Gaelic song under her breath.

John Murray ate hardly anything. He took a long time to find his coat and hat, and moved vaguely round the room, even though St Giles had struck the hour outside.

'You'll be late at Little Picardy,' Christine reminded him.

'Aye, I ken,' he replied irritably. He looked at the door.

'I was half-expecting –' he began, and his words trailed away as there was another tirl on the door-pin.

Mr and Mrs Lindsay entered. Mrs Lindsay looked upset, and her husband had a grave face.

By the way their glances crossed with John Murray's, Christine knew at once that they had heard all about what had happened to Lord Balmuir. She thought of Jamie's cut face, and wondered fearfully if they had also found out about their adventure at the inn.

'You'll forgie our early visit, John,' said Mr Lindsay. 'This business canna wait.'

Mr Lindsay cleared his throat. 'We'd like to hae a word with you alone.'

'Surely, surely,' said Murray. His face was grey and

bleary from lack of sleep. He pointed to his room. 'Christine –'

With surprising firmness Mrs Lindsay pushed Christine towards the stair door. 'I'll send Christine to step down the stair to our house for a while.'

'Let her go there,' said John Murray with a weary shrug. Christine was bewildered by the way in which her father let the Lindsays treat him, as if he had to clear himself of some grave accusation.

The rest of the family were not at all surprised to see her when she went down. Sophia was playing with Robin on the floor of the parlour. They smiled as she entered, then went back to their game. Old Mrs Lindsay sat hunched over her stick by the fire. 'Like an old witch,' thought Christine, but the eyes that turned towards her were kind, although a little exasperated.

'Eh, Christine, here's a bonny steer!'

'I ken,' she said in a low voice. 'Where's Jamie?'

'Inby,' snapped old Mrs Lindsay. She rapped her stick on the floor. 'Jamie!'

Jamie came in. He ran forward and took Christine's hands.

'Ah, well,' said Mrs Lindsay to the fireplace. 'I ken when the young folks dinna want me,' and she rose with creaking joints to go to her room. The children were still intent on their game with Robin's bricks; it was as if they had been left alone.

'Jamie,' said Christine anxiously, 'hae they heard about the letters, and our going to the inn?'

'Na, na,' he reassured her. 'I told them nothing. I said I had taken a fall on the stair.' He touched his cheek and winced. 'It's Balmuir they're fashed about. Dr Herries cried in to tell us. What happened after I left you?'

Christine explained how Ewan had come back to Davidson's Land; how she had gone to see Lord Balmuir with her father, and how Ewan had tried to seize the incriminating letter. At the end of her story, she yawned with exhaustion.

Jamie gently touched her hands. 'Christine, I've something to tell *you*. I wish it werena now, when there's so much other, but – well, I hae to go away.'

She went pale. 'When?'

'Tomorrow, to Pitcairnie. You mind, our family place in Fife. My sister Mary is ill, and my mother has asked me to go with her across the ferry. I canna say no.'

'Oh!' Christine's mouth quivered miserably, as she felt her last support being taken away. Jamie put his arm round her.

'It will be only a few days, until after the New Year.'

'Why does it hae to be just now?' she cried in despair. Jamie could not understand why she was so upset. 'You didna take on so when I told you I'd go to Leyden to study Dutch law next winter. That will be for a year, and it's miles across the sea.'

'That's different,' she wailed, 'and it's not so soon.' Then she tried to be sensible. 'I'll hae to live without you, I suppose,' she sighed, and put her head against his coat.

'You'll like me all the better,' he joked. Then he pulled her to her feet. 'My grandmother gied me a crown for my Christmas. She made me promise not to let on to the rest of the family. Christine, I'd like fine to buy you a present, if you'd let me.'

Suddenly she felt much more cheerful. 'Where shall we go with your crown?'

'Down to the Krames – I'll just tell my grandmother we're away out. We'll not be long. I ken just the very stall I want to take you to.'

When Mr and Mrs Lindsay returned to their own flat, Mrs Lindsay spoke in a kindly way to her, and Mr Lindsay patted her shoulder. At the door Jamie whispered that he would try to see her early next morning, before he went away.

Christine clutched his present tightly against her breast:
a small heart-shaped brooch surmounted by a crown. It
was only pewter, because the money his grandmother had
given him would not cover the cost of silver. People used
to wear them against witchcraft, Jamie said. Now they were
tokens of – well, of friendship and affection. Christine
laughed a little to herself, remembering how Jamie had
gone red when the stallkeeper had brought out his tray
of trinkets to show them, and had winked at her. She hoped
the memory would keep her spirits up all the dreary time
he was away; but as she left him to go upstairs, she felt
her heart would burst with grief.

She found her father sitting on the window-seat.

'Are you not going to work?' she asked him.

'I suppose so. But I'll not stay with the Linen Company
much longer. How can I go on working for Balmuir? It
sticks in my throat he didna tell me that he was going to
lease Strathdallin. Maybe he had a reason for *that* – but
as for turning Lady Strathdallin out of her house, he's a
villain to do it!'

Christine could not help hoping that there was some explanation.

'Father, why dinna you write to her, and find out what
has happened?'

He gathered himself together, as if she had suggested
the one thing to calm his disordered thoughts. 'Aye, I'll
write to Isobel. Then maybe I'll see my road clear.'

He appeared half an hour later with his great-coat on,
looking more cheerful. 'Christine, I hae made up my mind.
I'll bide with the Company until Lady Strathdallin comes
to Edinburgh. That will be the spring. Then I shall go
back to my old regiment in France. This place stinks in
my nostrils, after all this steer. Lord Balmuir is too big a
man for me to tangle with, and I might not hold my
tongue, if we went on seeing each other.'

'What will become of Lilias and me?' she cried in dismay.

He put his hand on her shoulder. 'I've asked Isobel to take you to live with her. Maybe she could come to this house, so you wouldna hae so much of a change . . . Will you miss me, Christine?'

She flung her arms round him, and pressed her head against his shoulder. 'You ken I will,' she said in a miserable voice, and almost begged him to take her to France with him. Yet behind the dismal thought of his going away, came another. She could not suppress the joy that rose with it. If she stayed in Davidson's Land, she could go on seeing Jamie.

'Maybe I shouldna hae asked such a daft question,' he said sadly. She looked up quickly, and realized that her father knew everything.

Jamie's good-bye next morning was a few hasty words in the doorway, as he went to find the hackney-coach that had been ordered to take his mother to the ferry. Christine tried not to spoil their few moments with tears, although she was tongue-tied with dejection, and could think of nothing to say.

'It's only a week,' he said, trying to sound cheerful. 'The carrier from Pitcairnie comes across to Edinburgh every seven days. If the roads dinna get blocked with snow, I'll send you a letter.'

His lips touched her cheek, then he waved, and ran down the stair. Christine went indoors. She did not want to see him again when he returned to escort his mother to the carriage. Their farewells must not be shared with anyone else, not even Mrs Lindsay.

The days crept drearily by until the New Year. On New Year's Eve, Christine heard noisy singing in the street; through a crack in the shutters, she saw a sea of lanterns and the upturned, grinning faces of people jostling up and down the Royal Mile as if it had been mid-day. She thought of the English travellers who had sung their Christmas carol round the horse-trough on December 25th. She had shared their excitement because she had been with Jamie; now the New Year merrymaking she had known all her life seemed foreign, because Jamie was miles away on the other side of the Firth.

The next morning, she took a bowl of calvesfoot jelly down to Lord Balmuir's house in the Canongate. She had a superstitious feeling that whatever she did on this important day would influence the rest of the year; she wanted to make some gesture of faith that Lord Balmuir had not really turned against her father and Lady Strathdallin.

Down in Crathie's Court, the flagstones had been thickly strewn with straw, and there was a rag swathing the tirling-pins on each of the doors. She knocked softly on Balmuir's door, and heard slow footsteps inside. Then Henrietta lifted the latch.

Her cousin seemed to have lost all her vivacity. She was pale-faced, and her hair was drawn severely back, without any curl. Christine looked down at the checked cloth tied over the top of her bowl of calvesfoot jelly. Somehow it now seemed foolish to have brought it.

'I brought this for your father,' she said, holding out the bowl. 'It's gey strengthening, and it's Lady Strathdallin's receipt.'

Henrietta's cold hands closed over her own round the bowl.

'How kind of you, Christine! Come away in, and we'll talk in my room.' Her voice fell to a whisper as they walked up the stair. 'You'll not be affronted if I dinna call my mother. She's sleeping now, and she has not had much rest since we came here.'

They sat on the bed which Henrietta shared with her sister, and drew the patchwork quilt up to their chins, because the fires were not lighted in the bedrooms until mid-afternoon. Elizabeth and Geordie had stayed behind at Balmuir House. Their mother wanted everything round Lord Balmuir to be as quiet as possible until he recovered.

After a while they stopped talking about Lord Balmuir. Henrietta's dull eyes began to sparkle, and she wriggled under the quilt as she told Christine about the dancing assembly she would attend for the first time in February. She giggled excitedly, and gradually both their voices became louder.

'Henrietta,' said a voice at the door. There was Lady Balmuir in a silk wrapper, with her undressed hair falling down her back. She smiled away Christine's apologies for disturbing her.

'I was hoping it would be you, my dear. Your father will be glad to hear that my husband is almost recovered, except for a stiffness in his shoulder. Dr Herries will not let him leave his room until next week, and he is weary for company, as he says. Would you come with your father on Sunday afternoon? He is a tiresome patient now, I can assure you.'

Christine repressed her dismay. She could not say what her father's present feelings towards Balmuir were. 'I will tell my father so, madam.'

'That will be delightful. He asks me to thank you for your jelly.' She hesitated a moment. 'I am not allowed to tell you, but I must say this – he has some news for you. It concerns a letter he has had from Lady Strathdallin.'

The hope in Christine's mind died as she saw Lady Balmuir's serious expression. The best that she could expect was that there would not be an open quarrel between her father and Balmuir.

When she gave him the invitation, he made a sour grimace. 'Hmph,' he snorted. 'I canna afford to offend him, so I suppose we'll hae to go.'

'Father –' she implored.

'I hae more sense now,' he reassured her. 'I'll not waste breath casting up my grievances at him. I'll be gey genty and civil. He'll never ken I've seen the lease on his desk.'

On Saturday evening he came home with three letters in his pocket. 'A fine expense the womenfolk put me to,' he grumbled jokingly as he produced them. 'I've had to pay three times over. Lady Strathdallin has written separately to Lilias, and here's another for you, Christine, from Fife.'

So Jamie had not been able to send a message through the carrier. Christine seized the single folded sheet, sealed with a great splash of wax that was imprinted with the arms of Lindsay of Pitcairnie. The letter was short, and rather solemn, but Christine read it twenty times. Again and again she returned to the last sentence: 'We shall come back to Edinburgh on Sunday.'

Lilias had retired to the kitchen with her letter. They could hear her spelling out the sentences to herself. Presently she came back to the parlour.

'Mr Murray,' she said, 'I am sorry to be telling you this, but soon I shall be quitting you. In this letter Lady Strathdallin gives me leave.'

'Will you so!' cried John Murray, half vexed and half amused. 'But hae *I* gien you leave, Lilias?'

Lilias smoothed the front of her apron. 'Och, sir, you must not torment me with such hard questions. You will mind that I was sent down to keep an eye on Miss Christine here. Now I am to be married, so I hae asked Lady Strathdallin to release me.'

John Murray smiled. 'At least, you can bide with us until the spring?'

'I think I might be able to pleasure you in that, sir,' said Lilias gravely, and returned to the kitchen.

John Murray went back to his letter. 'Heaven kens I canna make out any of Isobel's letters these days,' he complained. 'Here she says I am on no account to break with the Company until I hae seen Lord Balmuir. She speaks quite kindly of the man.'

On Sunday afternoon they walked down to the Canongate. Christine turned to stare at every coach that passed them, in the hope that she might see Jamie and his mother inside. It was one of those cheating days that come in the middle of winter: so sunny that the air feels warm and makes one forget that there are still three months of biting frost and sleet to be endured. The straw had gone from Crathie's Court, and a blackbird in a cage hung outside one of the windows to catch the sun. He sang and trilled as if the spring had come.

Christine was relieved to see that her father was showing none of his annoyance with Balmuir. Indeed, he seemed amused at her anxiety as they mounted the stair.

They were shown into the study where they had encountered Ewan. Lord Balmuir was wearing an undress gown lined with fur, that fell to his feet, and he was sitting in a chair by the fire. A bottle of claret and a snuff-box stood at his elbow. He was paler than usual, but otherwise seemed in good health. He stretched his hand towards them.

'You see me in better fettle than the last time,' he said.

'It pleases me, sir,' replied John Murray. Balmuir gave him a sharp look.

'You seem set on leaving us, I hear.'

'Sir?'

Balmuir gestured impatiently. 'Och, "sir", he cries me. I am your cousin Adam, John. Come here to the fire.' He put out his hand and pulled Christine down beside him. She was dismayed by the stern way in which her father bowed and sat with formal stiffness on the edge of the chair opposite Balmuir.

'It is true. I've taken the notion to go back to France. I hae asked Lady Strathdallin to look after Christine.'

'So she has told me.' His eyes glittered. 'So you no longer hae any notion of an estate of your own?'

John Murray flushed, but still kept a guard on his tongue. 'I dinna seem likely to come to one, so I am returning to my other trade.'

'You dinna think long to Tulmore?'

'You best should ken that, Balmuir!' cried Murray furiously. 'You that hae leased it with the rest of Strathdallin for yourself!'

Balmuir heaved himself out of his chair. 'Gie's your hand, John. I'll not torment you further. I couldna tell you sooner, since the business wasna right settled; but you should have learnt before the New Year, if this cursed shoulder hadna stopped me.'

The old man's eyes danced as he poured out two glasses of wine. Then he looked round at Christine, and poured a third. 'A wee one winna hurt her,' he said gleefully.

'Cousin Adam, tell us,' she begged. He was enjoying his secret so much it seemed he would never part with it. A reluctant hope began to struggle in John Murray's eyes.

'Here's the marrow of it,' said Balmuir. 'I hae leased the whole of Strathdallin. I hae taken such an interest in the district, it seemed the most sensible thing to do. But I dinna mean to bide there myself. Na, na, I shall stay on at Easter Balmuir. Maybe Geordie, if he ever comes to years of discretion, will hae the guiding of it – but not me.'

'What about Lady Strathdallin?' asked Murray suspiciously. 'Why is she to leave?'

'I am pulling down the wreck of the old house, for the old place isna fit to keep pigs in, and every winter it crumbles some more.'

'That's true!' put in Christine, remembering the leaky ceilings, and the wind that came in through the holes in the wall.

Balmuir went on: 'Lady Strathdallin approves, and it was her own idea that she should come to live in Edinburgh. Near the old foundations I shall put a small, decent place, not much bigger than the farmhouses that'll hae to be rebuilt from the tacksmen's houses. How else shall I hae the kind of tenants I need?'

'This small, decent place –' said John Murray slowly.

'I was coming to that.' Balmuir watched him with a sly look.

'I can only come to Strathdallin when I'm on the circuit,

or maybe in the summer vacation. I'll need a good factor
to run the estate when I'm not there. A man that kens the
place and the people well, John. Someone to push through
the new ways of guiding the land, and raise the growth of
flax. And above all, John, a man who would wink if aye
and on a wee bit of the rents found their way back to Lady
Strathdallin, and not into *my* pockets. Do you think I
could find such a body, John? Could you do the work
yourself?'

John Murray sprang to Balmuir's side and grasped his
hand.

'Sir, sir,' he cried joyfully, 'what can I say to thank you?
Och, cousin Adam . . .' He broke off, and to Christine's
alarm, looked as if he might burst into tears. Balmuir tact-
fully looked away until he could control himself, and
took Christine's hand.

'What about you, my doo? Will you go back to Strathdallin? I'd be loath to lose you.'

Christine looked at her father. Murray shook his head.
'I doubt I'll be away up there, long before the new house is
fit to live in. You'll hae to bide in Davidson's Land with
Lady Strathdallin, until the autumn, at least. Then maybe
both of you can –' He broke off.

'Imph!' Balmuir gave him a long, slow smile. 'What's
to become of Lady Strathdallin, then, when Christine goes
north?'

Murray stared at the floor, embarrassed but smiling
proudly.

'You can trust me to see to that. I'll take care of Isobel,
if she'll let me . . . I think she will.'

He glanced sideways at Christine. She smiled back happily, and took his arm.

Balmuir pointed to their glasses. 'Lift them up,' he
ordered. 'After the autumn, guid kens what might happen. Eh, John?' He threw Murray a teasing glance.

'You and I, John,' said Balmuir, 'hae a deal of business
to discuss. We'll not weary Christine with our dreich talk

today. The morn's morn will be soon enough.' He lifted his glass to John Murray.

'Your health, Tulmore!'

There was a clattering of hooves out in the street. Christine waved excitedly through the window. Mrs Lindsay came out of the carriage, then Jamie, who carried some luggage. He stood on the steps and looked up at Christine.

Breathlessly, she ran down to meet him, just as he was carrying the cloak-bags into the Lindsay's flat. He came out again on to the landing.

'Dinna go in,' she called. 'Jamie, Jamie, I've such a deal to tell you, and I'm so pleased to see you back again.'

He laughed and took her hands. 'Then we'll hae to jink the others, for there's no peace to talk in our house. Come up the Hill.'

They ran outside again, where Jeanie the pig looked up at them from the gutter, and Lucky Robertson waved at them through the open door of her shop.

'Jamie, you daft creature,' called down Mrs Lindsay, 'where are you away to?'

'Up the Hill,' he cried back. 'We'll not be long.'

They ran a hundred yards or so up the street, then had to slow to a walk, because the steepness took their breath away. Gasping, and laughing with delight, Christine told her news in jerky, unfinished sentences, until they reached the open ground in front of the Castle.

'So you're not going back to Strathdallin?' he said happily.

'Not until next autumn, at least.'

'That's when I go to Leyden,' Jamie said. 'Will you be here when I come back, Christine?'

They looked at each other anxiously, their thoughts moving into a future dark with separation. Then Christine breathed deeply, and smiled. Why, at that time – almost two immensely long years hence – she would be eighteen, and Jamie would be nearly twenty. As Balmuir had said to her father. 'Guid kens what might happen,' and Christine knew with certainty that in the end there would be no more separation.

'If I am away when you come back, Jamie,' she laughed, 'then –' She stopped, because what she was going to say sounded so foolish. But he would understand.

'Yes?' he said eagerly.

'You need only ask me to come back.'

Historical Note

ALL the speaking characters in this book are imaginary except for the officers who began the riot in the Canongate theatre.

Nevertheless, old Mrs Lindsay, Lord Balmuir, Ewan McDonnell, and many others – including Jeanie the pig – can be paralleled among the figures of the time. They can be found in Chamber's *Traditions of Edinburgh*, Cockburn's *Memorials of His Time*, and Kay's *Edinburgh Portraits*.

There was a 'Culloden riot', although it took place a little earlier than December 1751, and a Jacobite conspiracy of the kind I have described, known as the 'Elibank Plot', did take place in 1751–2.

I should like to offer my thanks to the official of the Saltire Society who answered my questions and showed me over the Society's headquarters in the Lawnmarket, so making it possible for me to write about 'Davidson's Land'.